Hamlyn Story Library
Fantastic Adventure
Stories for Boys

Hamlyn Story Library

Fantastic Adventure Stories for Boys

Selected and edited by
Leonard Matthews

Hamlyn

London · New York · Sydney · Toronto

First Published 1977
by The Hamlyn Publishing Group Limited
London · New York · Sydney · Toronto
Astronaut House, Feltham, Middlesex, England
© IPC Magazines Limited

ISBN 0 600 35245 5

Printed in Italy

Contents

Satellite One-Zero

Although a hundred years had elapsed since the first Moon flight, there would always be dangers to be faced in space travel. In spite of advanced equipment and nuclear powered spaceships, emergencies would still occur. This one was unprecedented. A Russian rocket armed with a nuclear war-head, fired into orbit sixty years previously and since then circling in space was now approaching Earth. . . .

A rogue rocket! Could anything prevent a cataclysmic disaster occurring on our planet?

'Sir! Could you come over here a minute?'

The clear voice of Space Cadet Jim Magister rang out across the cathedral-like silence of the radar dome making all the other young trainee astronauts look up from their work, and then glance apprehensively at Space Captain Straker, their bristly instructor in cosmic search techniques.

'Well, what is it, Magister? Have you discovered a new planet, or something?' The instructor's sarcastic tone of voice silenced the ripple of laughter that had begun amongst the other space cadets.

Jim Magister blushed with embarrassment as he turned away from his radar-scope console and faced Space Captain Straker.

'Well, er . . . not exactly, sir, but there is something strange in deep space. I've been tracking it for some time, and I can't identify it with any of the solar orbit tables.'

'Let me see your plot co-ordinates, lad,' growled the instructor. 'If my guess is correct, you've probably been making inaccurate azimuth readings. A common fault, that.' He grabbed the sheets of graph paper from the space cadet and ran his eye down the neatly written rows of figures. There was a moment's silence, and Jim Magister could sense all other cadets staring surreptitiously at him.

'Just as I thought,' snapped the instructor. 'You were observing with the simulator circuit switched in. You've been plotting one of the fictitious training programme orbits. Let's hope you don't make idiot mistakes like that when you are assigned to one of our satellite stations, Magister!'

The instructor flung the sheets of paper down on the desk beside the young cadet, and turned on his heel before Jim could say anything more.

The tall space cadet's face went red again. But this time it was with anger not embarrassment. He was one of the best pupils the Royal Space Academy had turned out, and he had a mathematical mind which, although it lacked experience, was superior to that of Space Captain Straker. The test instructor knew this and resented the boy. However, Jim Magister was not going to jeopardise his chances of graduating by losing his temper. He had worked too hard for that. Besides, there was only another day to go, and he would be able to wear his 1st Space Lieutenant's star on the epaulets of his sky blue uniform.

Later, when the radar practice session was completed, Jim walked across the parade ground with his friend and fellow space cadet, Rod Lester.

'Relax, Jim,' smiled his chum. 'Old "Strike-a-light" will be just a memory by this time tomorrow. Any mistakes we make after that will be our own look-out.'

'But I didn't make a mistake, Rod. I re-checked my figures and my circuit sequences. I certainly did not have the simulator in circuit. Those signals I plotted were real. There is something alien in deep space, about a million miles beyond Satellite One-Zero. I didn't get enough readings to make a conclusive orbit calculation, but it could be on a collision course with Earth.'

Jim's serious face convinced Rod that there was no point in treating the affair as either a joke or a mistake any more. He had too much respect for his pal to do that.

'All right, Jim. I believe you. How about going over Straker's head and telling the Commandant about it?'

The two of them were now abreast of the launching pads which formed a part of the Royal Space Academy. Jim looked across at the distant service gantries supporting the massive nuclear powered spaceships. Without turning his head, he spoke again.

'What's the point? He probably wouldn't listen, and anyway I haven't sufficient co-ordinates to be sure. It was such a small object I was only able to take intermittent fixes on it.'

Rod Lester smiled again. He didn't want Jim to be upset at this stage. Graduation day was too exciting an occasion to be gloomy about, and besides, they all had a lot of preparation to do that evening. Even in the year 2070 uniforms had to be clean and smart, and shoes polished!

Graduation day came and went, and in all the hustle and bustle the two friends hardly had time to exchange more than a few words.

The next time they met was outside the Commandant's office on the thirty-first floor of the administrative building two days after the graduation ceremony. After admiring each other's smart new uniform with its shining silver star on each epaulet, Rod Lester grinned happily.

'Well, Space Lieutenant Magister, and what are you doing outside the big white chief's office?' He paused, and as he remembered what Jim had been worried about on that last day in the radar dome, his face went serious. 'You haven't decided to tell him about that mysterious object in deep space you picked up, have you?'

Jim Magister smiled back at his chum. 'No, but I haven't forgotten about it. I'm here to receive my first posting to a satellite in space. I was ordered to report at 0900 hours. I also have a special request to make to the commandant. Something personal.'

'Okay, Jim. I won't ask any more questions. But I, too, was asked to report to the chief this morning at 0905 hours, and . . . .'

Before Rod could finish what he was saying, the door of the anteroom leading to the commandant's office was opened by his personal adjutant.

'Attention!' The adjutant's eyes swept over them, taking in every detail of their uniforms. Satisfied with their appearance, he gestured towards the door. 'All right. As you are both here the commandant will see you together. Inside, come along!'

The adjutant's sudden announcement had taken the pals by surprise, but they quickly recovered, and marched smartly through to the inner office.

The grey haired commandant's kindly eyes looked approvingly at the two smart young space lieutenants. On his desk was an open file. He was brief and to the point.

'Lieutenant Magister and Lieutenant Lester, I have decided to grant your requests for a joint posting.' They snatched a quick astonished glance at each other. . . . 'You will go on the next relief crew to Satellite One-Zero. Blast off will be at 19.30 hours tomorrow. Report to Captain Newcomb for briefing. That's all. Good luck to you both.'

When the chums were once more outside the commandant's office, they burst into laughter.

'You idiot,' chuckled Jim. 'Why didn't you tell me you were sending a request to be posted with me?'

'Why didn't **you**?' countered his friend, giving him a playful punch on the chest.

Still laughing, they emerged from the high-speed lift, and climbed into the little inter-camp hovercar. Then as they neared the Control Block, where Captain Newcomb had his quarters, Rod said: 'Wasn't that mysterious space contact of yours within radar range of Satellite One-Zero, Jim?'

Jim put the hovercar into reverse thrust to slow it down. 'Yes, it was. Their transmitter and receivers should be powerful enough to pick it up – if they search that segment.'

They left the hovercar and stood outside the Control Block for a moment. 'Don't you think it worthwhile telling Space Captain Newcomb about it? He's a much more reasonable chap than old strike-a-light Straker.'

Jim considered his friend's suggestion for a minute and then said: 'I will tell him, Rod, but not until we are aboard the satellite. Once we are up there I might get another chance to use their radarscope and re-check my readings. If I say anything to our new C.O. he might think I'm just trying to impress him, and anyway, he'd be bound to call Straker in to discuss it.'

Other members of the relief crew for Satellite One-Zero were arriving for the briefing, and Jim and Rod had no more time to discuss the problem.

The hours to blast-off slipped by rapidly. There were pre-flight medical checks to be gone through, space suits to be tested, and inter-planetary escape drill to be completed. Although a hundred years had elapsed since the first Moon flight, there would always be dangers to be faced in space travel; and in spite of their advanced equipment and nuclear powered spaceships, emergencies could still occur. Safety in space depended on eternal vigilance by the highly trained astronauts. The satellites, or space stations, operated by the various nations of the world were a vital part of that vigilance. Travellers to Mars, Saturn and other planets in the Solar system relied on information such as the positions of meteor clusters and cosmic dust clouds were essential to the pilots navigating their way across the orbital paths.

At blast-off-minus-fifteen-minutes, Jim and Rod were strapped in their seats, together with Space Captain Newcomb and three other crew members in the six-man capsule. Although they had made a number of orbital flights round the Earth during training, this was the first 'escape' flight the newly graduated space lieutenants had made. Satellite One-Zero was more than

5,000 miles out from Earth, but the trip would take them only a few hours.

Jim watched the digital clock ticking away the minutes and then the final seconds. Instinctively he closed his eyes as the huge rocket began to vibrate due to the tremendous power of the nuclear engines. Then, with a shuddering roar, the gleaming metal monster lifted off its launch pad, thrusting Jim back into his padded contour seat as it built up acceleration.

'Blast-off-plus-three! All systems green!'

The voice of Space Captain Newcomb reporting to base brought Jim back to full consciousness. The enormous G forces began to slacken off as the rocket reached its orbital velocity of 17,5000 m.p.h.

First, they had to make one orbit of the Earth, and make further flight checks before accelerating to the escape velocity of 25,000 m.p.h. at a precise pre-calculated moment. Jim and Rod had little to do at this stage except observe the more experienced crew members carry out their duties inside the capsule.

All was well, and soon, the motors re-started and gave the final stage of the rocket its extra boost. Behind them the Earth receded until they could see it as a gigantic glowing sphere hanging in the blackness of space. A beautiful and yet eerie sight.

An hour later, the huge wheel shape of Satellite One-Zero appeared on the forward TV screen. Slowly, skilfully, Captain Newcomb carried out the docking manoeuvre which brought the nose of the capsule into the outer airlock of the satellite, and one by one they entered.

The satellite's crew greeted them eagerly. A month in space can produce strange effects. A sense of loneliness, of being abandoned and cut off from Earth, sometimes made men who were ending their tour of duty almost hysterical. It was a symptom of space-sickness.

At last, Jim and Rod had some work to carry out. They were given the task of transferring the fresh supplies of food and water from the rocket to the satellite.

As soon as the transfer had been completed, and the old crew seen safely away in the rocket, Captain Newcomb allocated duties, and he readily agreed to Jim's request to man the radarscope.

Rod was ordered to man the computer, a position which was alongside the radar console so that any calculation needed by the radar operator could be made quickly.

An hour later, the huge wheel shape of Satellite One-Zero appeared on the forward T.V. screen.

Jim took the notes he had kept about the object he had seen from the training school radar dome from his pocket, and moved the remotely controlled external antenna towards the segment of the heavens where the object, he thought, might be now.

'Any response?' asked Rod.

'Not a thing . . . yet . . .' said Jim.

'Let me feed your co-ordinates into the computer. The orbit will be different from the orbit as it appeared from Earth.'

'Right,' replied Jim, and passed his notes over to his chum.

Quickly, Rod fed the information into the computer.

'There,' he said, passing a slip of paper over to Jim. 'Try that quadrant.'

Jim's fingers moved over his controls and after a few seconds he looked at Rod. 'There it is, look! It has quite a strong signal, and is less than half a million miles away. . . .'

Rod leaned over and peered into the hooded screen.

'That's good enough for me, Jim. Take some interval readings while I see Captain Newcomb. If your original calculations were correct, that thing, whatever it is, could reach Earth within a few days.'

By the time Captain Newcomb had returned with Rod, Jim had had time to plot the orbit of the mystery object, and he told his Captain the story of how he had seen the unidentified radar response from Earth.

'What puzzles me,' said Captain Newcomb, 'is why nobody else has reported this . . . let me see' . . . he pulled out a space manual from a rack above the radar console, 'ahh! yes Satellite 16 should be keeping that quadrant under observation . . . that's one of the Russians'. They should have reported it as a matter of routine. I wonder why. . . .'

As he spoke, Larry Fuller, the radio operator of the crew came on the intercom loudspeaker.

'Captain, message from Space Station 16. Russians request us to prepare to receive a ferry rocket immediately.'

'Right! Prepare the docking collar and the airlock,' ordered Captain Newcomb. His long experience and training told him that something pretty urgent must have made the Russians use one of their ferries to cross the void between the two satellites. The ferries were for emergency escapes, like lifeboats on an ocean liner. To use one in this fashion was very unusual.

Half an hour later, the tiny rocket nosed into the airlock, and a space-suited Russian emerged.

'I am Space Commandant Solikov,' he said, gripping Captain Newcomb's hand.

'Glad to meet you,' said Captain Newcomb. 'Now, what's all this about — or is it about the object on bearing two-seven-three amber quadrant?'

'Ah – so! You have picked it up,' said the Russian. 'Have you reported it to Earth?'

'Not yet,' answered the British astronaut.

A look of intense relief passed over the Russian's face. 'That is the best news I have had for a week. I must beg you not to say anything. I had better explain . . . .'

'Yes, you do that,' said Captain Newcomb. 'I don't like the sound of things.'

The Russian sat down, pale faced, and started to talk quickly.

'That object you have picked up. We have known about it for three days. We thought at first it was a large meteorite, but the signal was unusually strong for a meteorite. Then we calculated its orbit and checked it against our tables. Gentlemen, it is not a meteorite. It is a rocket . . . one of ours, and it carries a nuclear warhead . . . !'

Jim and Rod gasped with horror, but Captain Newcomb's grim expression did not change.

'But, Commandant Solikov, nuclear bombs were all destroyed fifty years ago. Your country signed the World Agreement along with everyone else.'

The Russian put his hands to his head in a gesture of weariness. 'Yes, yes, of course. This rocket is an old one which we fired into orbit sixty years ago, but it mis-fired and went into a deep space orbit round the Sun. We thought it would pass close enough to the Sun to be exploded by its heat, but it has been circling in space all these years and gradually coming closer. If it strikes the Earth . . . .'

It didn't need much imagination on the part of the British crew to realise the implications of what the Russian astronaut had told them, and they understood why he did not want a message sent to Earth. There could be panic, and Russians would be blamed for the terrible consequences of a nuclear explosion.

There was a moment's silence, and then Captain Newcomb spoke. 'A rogue rocket, eh? Well, it could and has happened to others. It's no use blaming anyone after all these years. What we must decide is how we can get rid of it.'

'I have a plan for that,' said the Russian, who now seemed more relaxed as he realised that Captain Newcomb was going to help him.

'There is a big asteroid orbiting across the path of Mars. It could shortly become a danger to spaceships going there. Your satellite is in the best position to intercept this old rocket. If we could re-orbit it to meet the asteroid . . . .'

Captain Newcomb interrupted him . . . . 'It could be used to destroy the asteroid, thus making a virtue out of necessity. An excellent idea, my friend, but a dangerous one. I can't order my men to carry out a task like that.'

'But you would accept a couple of volunteers, wouldn't you, sir?' It was Jim Magister who spoke. He and Rod had already held a whispered conversation with each other, and agreed to try to divert the rogue rocket.

Captain Newcomb looked at the two young space lieutenants.

'Well, it is certainly a job for a couple of fit men, and you two are probably the fittest on board . . . and I should need the experienced men here to make the calculations and radio the instructions to you.' He stroked his chin thoughtfully for a second. 'All right! You can have a go. It will mean using two of our precious escape vehicles, but we'll have to chance it.'

The satellite became a hive of activity as more careful observations were made of the position of the approaching rocket, and fed into the computer together with information which Commandant Solikov had brought with him about the asteroid and its orbit. After several hours of intensive work, Captain Newcomb was satisfied they stood a reasonable chance of pulling it off.

He gave Jim and Rod a careful briefing. 'Take four radio controlled emergency retro-rockets with you. You'll have to leave the capsules to attach them. Place them exactly where Commandant Solikov has shown you on his diagram, and whatever you do, don't touch the trigger mechanism behind the warhead!'

A few hours later, Jim and Rod slipped separately into the emergency escape airlock, and entered the escape ferries. A crossbeam of radio pulses from the Russian and British space stations enabled them to enter an orbit which would bring them close to the menacing rocket.

Keeping in sight of one another, they moved silently across the void. Both their minds were filled with unanswered questions. Would their fuel be sufficient to return to the satellite? Would the rocket be damaged in any way after its long stay in deep space?

Jim anxiously watched the small radar screen in the escape capsule. He glanced across at Rod and saw him slowly rotating his capsule to widen the area of search. Suddenly his voice crackled over the radio. 'Jim! I've got it . . . ten degrees above us. Range reducing!'

'Contact! Well done, Rod.'

All their recent training in manoeuvring and docking came into use as they eased their way gingerly towards the sixty-foot long rocket with its lethal nose cone. When they were about fifty feet away, Jim sealed his spacesuit and, keeping himself tethered to his capsule, moved cautiously over to the rocket while Rod relayed instructions.

His task of fixing two of the retro-rockets finished, Jim regained his capsule while his pal moved out to attach his two. When all four were securely in position, Rod took a single cable connecting them, back to Jim's capsule and joined it to an external telephone communication socket.

'Hurry it up, Rod! Your suit-oxygen is running low,' Jim called over the radio. Rod's helmet vizor was beginning to steam up with all his exertions. He needed to retain his capsule before it fogged over completely and left him 'blind'.

'Lift a bit, Rod – take it easy. You're almost in line with your hatch.' Jim watched anxiously as his friend clambered clumsily back into his capsule, and breathed a sign of relief as he saw him close the hatch behind him.

The final task was to take accurate astral readings against stars in the galaxy.

Then, from his control panel in his capsule, Jim fired first one retro-rocket and then another on the Russian space bomb until it was in the correct position to be sent into its new orbit to intercept the asteroid.

'Right! Fire all rockets full power!' The instruction came from Captain Newcomb.

Jim obeyed, and watched as the space bomb shot away trailing the now broken cable. Within seconds it had vanished, and he and Rod re-orbited towards Satellite One-Zero.

Safely back on board they watched in the direction of the Mars orbit, shielding their eyes with space goggles.

'If we haven't made any mistakes with our calculations,' said Captain Newcomb quietly, 'we should see the explosion within the next ten minutes.'

The minutes ticked by, and Commandant Solikov suddenly shouted for joy. A bright orange glow like a small meteorite burning up at the upper edge of the atmosphere, flared briefly against the blackness.

'Strike a light!' cried Rod. 'We've done it. Smack on target.'

'We've done it all right,' grinned Jim, 'but do you have to mention that man's name at a moment like this?'

The Bad Men

Ed Dolan had been marshal of Crewsville, Arizona, for twenty years and his gun-hand wasn't as fast as it had been in the days of his youth. All his life he had fought bad men and Indians and his courage was still unimpaired. But he knew he was no match for the three riders who came to town to rob the bank.

But an ally was at hand. A kid named Johnny.

Crewsville, Arizona, lay sleepy in the hot sun. Young Johnny Mulford sat with Ed Dolan outside the Marshal's office. Ed was old now and had been Marshal for twenty years. He sat whittling a stick and smoking his old pipe.

'Nothin' ever happens around here,' Johnny was complaining.

'That's the way I like it,' Ed Dolan said. 'Not like the old days when I tamed this town. You took no more notice of a gun goin' off than you did a dog barking.'

They looked up at the sound of horses' hoofs in the dust and saw three riders enter town. They came slowly down the wide street and stopped their horses outside the *Lucky Chance* saloon.

'Strangers,' Johnny said.

Ed Dolan smiled grimly and said: 'So nothin' happens around here. Son, those boys are bad and they mean real trouble.'

'You know them, Marshal?' Johnny asked.

'Sure do,' the lawman said. 'That's Luke Haines and his two partners. They're the worst poison in this territory.'

They watched the three dismount from their horses and enter the saloon. Slowly Ed got to his feet. His face was pale under its tan. Johnny knew that the old man was scared. And he never thought to see the Marshal scared. Why, the old man was a hero of the frontier and had fought bad men and Indians all his life. The Marshal hitched his gun up on his hip and stepped down from the sidewalk.

'What're you goin' to do?' Johnny asked.

'Tell 'em to get-a-goin',' the old man replied. 'I ain't havin' that kind in my town. No, sir!'

Johnny said: 'You can't tackle the three of 'em, Marshal. They'll kill you!'

The old man looked at him and said: 'That's what I'm paid for, I reckon.' He started across the street and Johnny went to follow him: 'Stay where you are, son, this ain't somethin' a kid can mix in.' He eased his gun in its holster and walked across the street in the direction of the saloon. The boy stayed where he was for a moment and then followed him. Ed was his friend and he wasn't going to see him in trouble with nobody to help.

Nothing stirred in the town, the street was deserted in the noon heat. The Marshal stepped up on to the sidewalk and hesitated at the saloon door. Then he went inside. Johnny hurried to the door and peered in.

Three men were leaning against the bar. They faced the Marshal and they were grinning widely. The one in the centre, a big man with a broken nose and a scar down one cheek, said: 'Run along and play, old man, we ain't in the mood for jokes.'

'Now listen to me, Luke Haines,' the Marshal told him. 'I'll tell you once and I'll not tell you again. I don't want you in my town. Get on your horses and ride out, all three of you.'

Behind the three men, Johnny could see the barman's frightened face. The bad men were chuckling now. Luke Haines put his hand on his gun and said: 'You're scarin' the daylights out of me, Marshal. An' when I'm scared, I start shootin'. You'd better look out.'

The Marshal's hand hovered over the butt of his own gun.

'Take that hand off your gun,' he said.

Another man, wearing two low-slung guns, suddenly drew one and asked innocently: 'How about me? Am I allowed to draw one?'

As the Marshal turned towards him, Luke Haines pulled his gun out and levelled it at the Marshal. The third man hooted with mirth and drew his own gun. The Marshal stood very still, facing the three guns. Johnny thought he would turn away then, but the old man wasn't finished yet.

'I'm givin' you fair warnin',' he said. 'You either ride out of town or you get put in jail.'

Luke Haines raised his gun and fired. The bullet whisked past the startled Marshal's head and then smacked into the woodwork right by Johnny's head. The boy ducked and ran forward, yelling: 'You put those guns away. You can't do this in our town.'

They were laughing before Johnny appeared, now they seemed helpless with laughter. Luke Haines held his side with one hand and staggered towards the Marshal. He took the lawman's gun from him and threw it across the room and looked down at the boy who faced him so fearlessly.

One of the men said: 'We have a tough one here, Luke. Shucks, everybody around here scares me.'

That made them laugh some more. Then Luke Haines faced the Marshal and said: 'Get back into your hidey-hole, Marshal an' stay there if you know what's good for you.' He jerked a thumb at Johnny. 'And take this durned kid with you.'

Johnny flung himself at the outlaw who cuffed him so that he ran into another man.

'Throw him out, Bill,' Haines ordered. 'And this old fool, too.'

The man called Bill, who had a black beard and a squint in one eye, took hold of Johnny by the scruff of his neck and the seat of his pants and carried him to the door. He kicked the door wide, stepped on to the sidewalk, and threw him into the street. The boy landed hard and had most of the wind knocked out of him, but he jumped to his feet and glared back at the laughing man.

'You won't get away with this,' he shouted, and the man laughed all the more.

Now Luke Haines and the other man appeared dragging the Marshal with them and flung him after Johnny. People had started to come running at the sound of the shot. They stopped when they saw the men with guns in their hands. Johnny helped the Marshal to his feet. Several of the citizens started towards the men outside the saloon, but they fired into the ground at their feet and drove them back. Luke Haines lifted his hand for silence. The angry shouting stopped.

'Listen to me,' he said. 'We're takin' over this town for a while an' the sooner you get that into your heads the better. Behave yourselves and nobody'll get hurt. Now go home.'

Slowly, under the menace of the guns, they went. Johnny walked with the Marshal back to his office. The old man sat down behind his desk looking tired and defeated.

'I'm finished,' he said. 'I've been disgraced in front of the whole town.'

'No, you haven't,' Johnny said. 'We haven't even started yet. We'll show 'em.'

The old man looked up, puzzled.

'What're you talkin' about, son?' he said. 'There's three outlaws with guns in the saloon. What can we do?'

'Just wait a bit,' said Johnny with a grin. 'You'll see.'

The outlaws stayed for two days and they took the town over all right. They swaggered the streets together and there wasn't anybody in town who dared to say 'no' to them. They helped themselves to anything they wanted in the stores, ate in the best restaurants and drank to their heart's content at the *Lucky Chance* without paying a cent for anything they had. They insulted respectable citizens and for fun made the parson dance on Main Street as they fired shots near his feet. They helped themselves to the best horses in the livery stable and looked like they had settled in for good. But they hadn't, of course. They had come for a purpose. They thought that nobody knew that purpose, but they were wrong. Johnny Mulford knew.

It was like this. Like most boys in town, Johnny knew that the saloon was raised slightly off the ground. He had played under there many times. It wouldn't be easy for a grown man to get under, but for a slender boy, it was easy. And he had spent most of the last two days, while the outlaws were in there drinking, listening to what they had to say. And they said a lot. Mostly how they were going to rob the bank. They planned to do it on their second night in town. But they didn't know what Johnny had in store for them.

It all started on that second night when Moose Davis, the third man of the trio, who was short and fat, sat down in the saloon's best chair. Johnny, who had been busy while the three of them were out eating, grinned in the darkness under the saloon as he heard the rending crash from above. He had sawn almost completely through one of the legs of the chair. The other two thought it very funny and laughed drunkenly. Moose didn't. He staggered to his feet with a roar.

'What's so durned funny?' he shouted. 'One of you varmints done that o' purpose.'

It took them ten minutes and another drink to calm him down. But as soon as he was quiet, the second 'accident' happened. Bill Dooley, the man with the beard, sat down at a table, still shaking with laughter over that chair giving way under Moose's bulk. He stopped laughing when Johnny, who had crept out from his hiding place and climbed quickly on to the roof to the skylight directly above Bill's position. It was the work of a minute to empty a bucket of water over the man below. He gave a scream of horror and leapt to his feet, drenched through to the skin. In a moment, Johnny was down from his perch and back under the floorboards to hear the end of the comedy. Bill was dancing around in an insane rage, yelling that everybody knew he hated water. This time Moose laughed a lot, so did Luke Haines.

Then suddenly Luke stopped laughing.

'Somebody's doin' this to us,' he drawled in a menacing voice.

The wretched, dripping Bill Dooley stared at him and asked: 'Who?'

'I don't know, but I'll soon find out,' the leader told him and hurried to the door. Under the floor, Johnny stuffed his hand in his mouth to stop the laughter.

Luke reached the door all right, but he didn't get any further, not on his feet, that is. The rope stretched across the doorway caught at his ankles and he hurtled across the sidewalk and landed with a loud thump in the street. Moose was close behind him and too foolish to stop, so the same thing happened to him. Just as Luke was getting to his feet. Moose's great weight caught him in the middle and put him back in the dust again.

Luke staggered to his feet cussing the air blue.

'Why in tarnation don't you look where you're going?' he shouted.

Moose shouted back. 'Don't you talk to me that way, wooden-head.' Luke swung a punch at him and they slogged it out on the street until Bill Dooley, still dripping water, came and parted them.

'Stop fighting,' he howled. 'Somebody's doin' this to us and we have to find 'em.'

That sobered them a little. They went back into the saloon and had some more drinks.

Luke Haines said: 'I don't like the way things're goin'. I reckon it's time to crack the bank and get out of here.'

The other two nodded and agreed. Moose rose and said: 'I'll go get the horses.' He walked out of the saloon, going very gingerly because he thought he might fall over a rope or a bucket of water might be emptied over him. He hated water as much as Bill Dooley did. But he got the horses safely and brought them to the hitching rail outside the saloon and tied them up. No sooner was he inside the saloon, than Johnny came out of his hiding place, opened his clasp knife and got to work on the saddle girths. The outlaws were in for a big surprise as soon as they started for the bank.

They came out of the saloon, hitching up their gun-belts, preparing themselves for the ride along the street to the bank. It would be easy to rob in the dark with few people about. They untied their horses and started to mount. Poor Moose! As soon as the stirrup-leather took his great weight, the cut girth gave way. Moose came back to earth on his heels with a jolt that jarred him from head to toe. He stood like a man stunned. As Bill Dooley swung *his* leg over the saddle, *his* girth gave way. He fell heavily to the ground with his foot still in the stirrup. He tried to get to his feet and the heavy saddle came down and caught him on the nose. Sleepily, he lay back in the dust.

Luke Haines stayed in the saddle a little longer. But not much. He managed to sit astride, but as his horse turned to leave the hitching rail, the girth gave way and he toppled sideways. He foolishly clutched at the saddle and went with it. He landed on Moose and they went down in a tangle of arms and legs. Moose yelled and got to his feet. When he bent down to help Luke up, Bill's horse kicked him in the seat of his pants and he went down again.

Bill Dooley, dazed by the blow from the saddle, got to his feet and wandered around in a circle until he trod on Luke's hand. That started a fight.

Johnny, still hidden under the saloon, and witnessing all the fun, hugged himself with delight.

Moose parted the two combatants and the three bad men now drew their guns and went looking for whoever had played the tricks on them. They didn't have much luck, because everybody seemed to know what was afoot, and stayed indoors. The three didn't think to look under the saloon. After they had hunted around for a while, they went into the saloon for another drink and there decided that if they were going to rob the bank and ride out of town, they would have to have more saddles.

They now led their horses to the livery stable, held up the old liveryman and helped themselves to some fresh saddles. When their horses were ready, they rode them in the direction of the bank. They were nervous now, and had their guns in their hands. They didn't know what to expect next.

While they were at the livery stable, Johnny slipped out of his hiding place and ran as fast as he could to the Marshal's office. He found the old man sitting sadly behind his desk.

'Mr Dolan,' Johnny said, 'I think it's time you came with your rifle. It's about now you should take Luke Haines and his gang prisoners.'

The Marshal jumped to his feet in surprise.

'What're you talkin' about, young 'un?' he demanded.

With a wide grin, Johnny told him: 'I've been softening 'em up a little.

They ain't so full of fight now.'

The wondering Marshal went and fetched his rifle and loaded it. Demanding to know what it was all about and not receiving any reply from the youngster, he followed Johnny out on to the moonlit street. There was an alleyway near the bank and into this the man and boy went and hid themselves. In a few minutes they heard the sound of horses' hoofs.

'Here they come,' said Johnny.

The three outlaws came in sight, Luke Haines in the lead. They still had their guns in their hands and they looked mean and dangerous. Johnny reckoned that they wouldn't be dangerous for long.

The men dismounted from their horses and tied them to the sidewalk railing. Then Luke said: 'Moose, you stand guard here. Bill and me'll go around the back.'

Johnny's heart missed a beat. He hadn't reckoned on them going in the rear way and had spread the sidewalk in front of the main entrance thick with axle grease. Sadly he watched the two men walk around the bank. He heard them breaking in the door and going inside. Five minutes later came the muffled *boom* as they blew open the safe. Then the fun began.

At the sound of the explosion, Moose jumped up on to the sidewalk and started towards the door. His feet no sooner touched the grease-smeared planks than they flew from under him. He hit them with a noise that could be heard all over town. His yell would have awakened the dead. He dropped his gun and it went off with a roar. He yelled a lot more then, because he had shot himself in the foot.

Howling, he struggled to get to his feet, managed to gain them, took one limping step and went down again.

Alarmed by the shot, Luke and Bill came running through the bank and wrenched open the door. Luke was in the lead. He jumped on to the sidewalk a thud that shook the whole building. He dropped his gun and it went off. This shot caught the unfortunate Moose in the seat of his pants. He yelled again and told the whole world that he had been murdered.

Bill, who followed close behind Luke, went sailing over his leader, clean into the street. Here he got entangled with the horses, which were rearing and kicking at the sound of the shots.

Luke tried to get up and went down again, this time landing on his chin. Carefully, he sat up, told Moose to shut his noise and demanded that Bill come and help him to his feet. Bill got himself out from among the horses and came running to his leader's aid. He jumped up on to the sidewalk and his feet flew higher than his head. Instead of helping Luke up, he landed on top of him and squashed him flat. The night was split with their howls and curses.

Johnny said to the Marshal: 'I think this is a good time to finish it, Mr Dolan.'

The old man grinned and agreed. He came out of cover with his rifle in his hands and called: 'Put up your hands! You're under arrest!'

Luke threw Bill from him and dived for his gun. He slid like a man on ice and banged his head against the wall of the bank. Seeing stars, he got groggily to his knees. Bill Dooley got to his feet and put his hands up so quickly that he lost his footing and sat down again with a loud thud.

But this time, people had come running. They came in time to see three crestfallen bad men arrested without a protest by an old man with a rifle and a young boy without any weapon at all.

'Marshal,' one of the townspeople said, 'you're a hero.'

'Not me,' said the old man. 'It was Johnny. He whittled 'em down to size and I just took 'em in.'

'Three cheers for Johnny,' somebody called, and with the cheers of the people ringing in his ears, Johnny walked with the Marshal and the three prisoners to jail.

Boy in the Big Wheel

*Martin hadn't done very much towards the glory of his school but now his big chance
had come. Stidger, famed for his inventions – the ice-yacht which had plunged through
ice into water, the booster-rocket which went up in flames, the go-kart which had
crashed on the headmaster's drive – had now come up with the gyrobike.*

*The Aeronautical Society had offered a prize of £5,000 for the first group to fly a
man-powered plane for a mile. Stidger had decided that he and his pals were going to
win that £5,000 – and Martin was going to fly the gyrobike!*

When they had untied Martin's blindfold he blinked several times, then bent
down to inspect where his shins – torn by brambles – were bleeding.

He was in thick woodland. The tree trunks grew straight and smooth to a
heavy canopy of branches far overhead.

'This way!'

The smallest of the three figures round him pointed through the trees, and
they side-stepped past the pines to an exceptionally large tree. Way-up –
about 30 feet Martin judged – its branches started to form in a cluster, black
against the sky.

It looked completely unclimbable.

'Shall I go up first to-day, Stidge?' It was the tallest boy who spoke.

'Okay, Frank,' said the small figure, peering through thick spectacles at a
clanking mass of metal he was rooting out from a thicket. 'Only don't fall off
like you did last time, you chump.'

The third youth, who had a straight cut fringe, laughed.

'Shut up, Bennett,' said Frank, looping two thin metal bands of the contraption round the trunk. 'Want everyone to hear us?'

Martin watched spellbound. On the two bands were two large pedals. Frank stood on these and started to climb the trunk. As he lifted each foot, as he would in going upstairs, the transfer of his weight tightened the bands round the tree trunk.

'What on earth is it?' said Martin as Frank reached the high-up branches.

'A tree-bicycle – foresters use them, but this is my own special design.'

'Do I have to climb on it?' asked Martin, trembling. He knew only too well of Stidger's outrageous inventions coming to sticky ends.

'No – just the first one up. Then he chucks down the – *watch out!* Here it comes.'

A rope ladder snaked down from the branches.

Bennett began to climb up its rungs.

'What are those?' Martin pointed to pieces of yellow-painted metal showing under a tarpaulin on which Stidger was sitting.

'100 cc chainsaws – but they belong to the school's forest gang; you know, those chaps who are going to clear away a lot of these trees. Right, your turn now.'

Martin gulped. He had seen this coming. It was always the same whether he was just going in to bat, about to receive the ball on the soccer field or face an exam – total fright!

'I – I can't. I get dizzy.'

Stidger shrugged. 'Frank,' he shouted. 'Lob down the rope so Martin can tie on to one end, then you pull it up as he climbs.'

Martin climbed fast to make up for his show of weakness. So fast that at the branches – *ouch!* – he hit his head on something hard. There were planks nailed just above. And he found himself squeezing through a tiny trapdoor.

'Watch where you step,' commanded Bennett moving a box of spanners out of the way.

'This is fantastic – *fantastic*,' said Martin.

It was. Branches had been cleared above the planks, and the space had been walled and roofed with sacking. On the floor lay strips of metal, bits of old bicycle, tools, things looking like model aeroplane wings. The place reeked of aircraft dope.

And in the centre of all this . . .

It was a large cage of alloy strips bolted together. Inside this was a big wheel, and inside this – its wheels resting in a deep groove in the rim of the big wheel – a bicycle.

There was a wooden aeroplane propeller at the front.

'You'd better not say anything about this to a living soul, or . . .' said Frank threateningly.

'No, no – but what is it, for heaven's sake?'

'Stidge'll tell you when he gets up the ladder.'

Martin's thoughts raced. *Why* had Stidger approached him yesterday saying: 'Hey, Martin, you haven't done much for your house or the school, have you? Well, now's your big chance. My gang want you to help us tomorrow.'

Stidger appeared through the trapdoor. 'Right,' he said. 'This is a gyrobike.'

'A gyrowhat?'

'Gyro*bike*. You sit on that bicycle and pedal like mad, and that makes the big wheel spin round and round. Right? Now you see the wire round the big wheel? It goes round a pulley on the propeller too, so that when you pedal the prop spins, and – Bingo! – you're flying!'

'Only if you've got the rotors on, too,' grunted Frank, tightening an awkward bolt.

'Ah,' said Stidger, 'yes.' He jerked a foot at the two long rotor-type wings on the floor. 'These spin round on the top of the gyrobike, on that axle.'

'Like a helicopter?' said Martin incredulously.

'A bit, but these rotors freewheel – it's the propeller that's doing the pulling, and the rotors act like moving wings and – ' He explained how the rotors fitted on the top.

Martin broke in. 'But it must have taken ages to build. Why didn't you do it in the metal workshop at school?'

Stidger's team grinned.

'£5,000 – that's why,' said Frank. 'That's the prize offered by the Aeronautical Society for the first group to fly a man-powered plane for a mile. *We're* going to do it.'

'Yes?' said Martin. 'I'm still mystified.'

Stidger polished his thick spectacles, then put them back on.

'All these trees are being cut down on Wednesday – two days away, so we *have* to get the thing flying by then . . .'

'So that's why the chainsaws are down there. But where do I come in?' Martin's voice went up to a squeak.

'We want you to fly it!'

'*EH?*'

Martin's world rocked. He staggered back forgetting for a moment the plunge into space through the sack walls. Frank caught his arm. Had he heard correctly?

'M-M-Meeee?'

'There's no one at Radton who does as much cycling as you,' said Stidger simply.

Which was true enough, thought Martin. His one claim to a forceful performance in anything was his cycling. Using a racing-style bike he toured the countryside for miles, and even rode 200 miles home for the holidays, then back again for term time.

A horrifying thought struck him. 'Y-You d-don't want me to fly it from *here,* do you?' He pointed at the floor.

Bennett and Frank sniggered.

'Come off it,' said Stidger. 'I'm not that mad.'

Martin wasn't so sure as he remembered past projects of Stidger's: the ice yacht which plunged through ice into the water; the booster-rocket which went up in flames; the go-kart which had crashed on the headmaster's drive.

Stidger had drawn back some of the sacking to show a wire hawser running from the hide-out gently down into the trees. A pulley on the gyrobike was arranged on top of the wire.

He was saying: 'No, we push the gyrobike off and let it slide down this wire to the ground, then you try to fly it there, and – '

'*Sssshhh!*'

Bennett pointed to the trapdoor. All four dropped to their knees, peering through cracks in the planks. 'Runters,' whispered Frank.

Down on the forest floor five youths were stalking through the undergrowth. The leader was large, and blond-haired. Snatches of talk drifted up to the hidden boys . . .

'*Stidger was coming this way . . . can't just vanish . . . wait till we find . . . hide-out . . .*'.

Stidger's team held their breath.

Then the quintet lumbered off into the woods with all the quiet of stampeding elephants.

'Phew,' said Stidger, 'Glad they didn't spot us. He's the last bloke we want to find us.'

Runters (nicknamed *The Blond Giant*) was a troublemaker. He plagued Stidger, but could never find his hide-out. And he was outmanœuvred time and again by the wily bespectacled 'inventor'.

Martin groaned inwardly. Now he was in the thick of gang warfare too.

Runters often picked on him, and if he got to know that Martin knew Stidger's secret . . .

'Want to fly the gyrobike?' said Stidger.

'What if I can't make it fly?'

'You just better had,' murmured Frank.

'Shut up,' said Stidger to his surly colleague. 'It was my idea to ask you, Martin. *I'm* sure you can do it. OK?'

Speech failed Martin. He dreaded failing yet again. He'd simply be more of a laughing stock.

'Take it or leave it.' Stidger sounded cool, and Martin felt the pleasure of being in with the gang slipping away.

'All right,' he said. 'When do we try?'

'Day after tomorrow.'

They climbed back down the rope ladder – except Frank, who was last man. He pulled up the rope ladder when the others were down, and then treadled the tree bike down the trunk.

'Better blindfold him,' said Bennett, jerking a thumb at Martin.

'No need,' said Stidger tersely. 'He won't split now.' Frank snorted but didn't say anything more. Silently they threaded a way back through the tall trees to school.

Waking next morning, Martin was astonished when it all came back to him. Had it really happened? Was he really so involved in this fantastic-sounding episode? He shivered at the thought.

Things were to become even worse.

At morning break-time, Martin felt his ear gripped in strong fingers. They belonged to Runters.

'Hallo, young 'un. Been walking in the woods lately, then?'

'What d'you mean?'

'Been taking strolls through Bishop's field and Brierley woods, then?'

'Let go – you're hurting.'

'Diddums,' sneered The Blond Giant. 'Liar. Saw you last night with Stidge, so don't tell fibs or . . .' He gave Martin's arm a sharp twist. Then his tone changed. 'Come on, then – where is it?'

'What?'

'The famous Stidge hide-out, fall-out shelter or wherever he does his mad experiments – well? I'll make it worth your while if you tell.'

He broke off as he saw Stidger approaching.

'Hey, Stidge, this chap's just told me about your HQ. What about that, eh? Can I join your gang now, Stidger?'

Martin cringed at the jeering tone.

'I didn't tell him anything,' he retorted, but Stidger looked blank-faced. 'Shut up, Runters,' he said. And then he turned to Martin. 'I'll sort you out later,' he said.

Left alone, Martin felt desperate. Who'd believe him? Martin the Mug! It was even worse when he found a note pinned inside his desk lid saying: *'Be at tree at 7. Watch you're not followed. S.'*

Heart sinking, Martin muttered: 'This is it – court martial!' He saw Bennett and Frank later at lunch, but they scowled and looked away.

After a roundabout walk Martin reached the tree. He had kept glancing behind but saw no one. The ladder was dangling down from the hide-out.

'Hallo?' he called.

Silence.

Gritting his teeth he started to climb the swaying ladder, not daring to look down. He felt terrified without the protection of the rope that had been tied on him before – but he soon reached the branches.

'Anyone there?' He stuck his head through the trapdoor. Silence again. The gyrobike stood neatly on the floor, now clear of all the tools and dope tins. Oil had been applied recently to the axles, and it trickled down the frame. The rotors were packed inside the frame.

The silence seemed sinister.

Suddenly a branch snapped below on the ground.

'Found it now, eh?' came a shout.

Martin quailed, looking down on a blond head.

'Oh! heavens, it's Runters!'

'Thanks for showing me the way,' yelled the figure. 'Stidge *will* be pleased with you – leading *me* here! I'm coming up . . .'

The ladder twanged as the boy trod the first rung. Quick as a bird, Martin pulled out his pen-knife and sawed at the ropes. There was a crash and a yell as the ropes parted.

'I'll get you for this,' came an angry voice.

Martin suddenly realised that he couldn't get down by the ladder now, but he was past caring.

Drrrrrr . . . 'Great Scott,' said Martin. 'The chainsaws – he's starting one up.' The two-stroke engine whirred healthily.

And as Martin gazed down, wooden chips started to fly from the tree trunk. There was no doubt about it. Runters was going to bring the tree down.

Martin ripped down the sack walls. The gyrobike was still attached by pulley to the wire cable snaking into the trees. Then he noticed a coil of rope tied to the machine.

He pushed the gyrobike into space. It lurched heavily down the wire as he paid out the loosely coiled rope over a branch to slow his load's progress.

Drrrrr . . . Runters seemed unaware of the freight being shipped down the high wire. He was making such a row.

Martin felt the gyrobike come to a stop in the distance. Must be on the ground, he thought. His fright had gone. Now he saw something else – a pulley and rope loop on the planks.

Fixing the pulley on the wire, he worked the loop under his armpits, took a deep breath and – jumped. *Whoosh!* He shot down the wire, braking by grabbing foliage on the way.

He seemed to fly miles instead of 70 yards. Then ahead he saw the gyrobike hanging a foot from the ground at the edge of the wood, where the cable was anchored to a tree. Shunting gently into it, Martin dropped to the ground.

The chainsaw had stopped. But crashings came from the wood. *Pursuit!* Martin clambered on the gyrobike and found the pulley release – a large wing nut.

Unscrewing this, he leapt clear as the machine clumped to the ground. 'Rotors next,' he muttered, yanking them out of the cage and slotting them on the top spindle – as Stidger had shown him the day before.

'Over here!' he heard someone yell.

Quick! He squeezed into the cage after checking the prop was facing the open field, and started to pedal, standing on his toes, sprint-style.

Faster and faster. His feet spun. So did the prop in a big silver circle with a thrashing sound. Head down, gripping the insulating tape-wrapped hand grips, he urged the machine forward across the grass.

'They won't get Stidge's plane,' he gritted, making a superhuman effort. A haze misted his eyes. Sweat poured off him. But he had the machine inches off the ground . . .

The big wheel whirred. The alloy cage frame shook. The rotors windmilled. The prop whined . . . and Martin was oblivious of them all.

In his imagination he was cycling flat-out down a long, straight and smooth road. Very fast! Suddenly a hedge crossed his path . . . *and he flew straight over it! Faster! Faster yet.*

'Martin!'

Stidger's voice! He stopped pedalling. The gyrobike dived shallowly back to earth. Martin slumped, exhausted.

Stidger and Bennett and Frank were crowding round, saying: 'Fabulous

. . . greatest . . . way-out . . . £5,000.' Shaking his hand and slapping his back.

'Where's Runters?' he gasped at last.

'Runters? – Oh, that!' said Frank looking very sheepish, and shaking flour out of his whitened head. 'That was old Stidge's masterplan. I pretended to be Runters, sawing down the tree and all that, hoping you would get the gyrobike to fly. *And you did.*'

'Give us an encore, Martin,' Stidger insisted, after he had had a long breather.

'Okay.'

He spun the propeller in zooming revs. The man-plan waddled forwards but, try as Martin could, the wheels refused to leave the ground.

'Let me try, Martin,' said Frank. 'I'm fresh.'

But he fared far worse, and couldn't even raise power to taxi the gyrobike. Neither could Stidger or Bennett.

They tried and tried and tried. But no one could produce the superhuman effort again.

'Well, one day, perhaps,' said Stidger, scratching his head ruefully, glaring at the mass of metal in the middle of the field.

'What are we going to do with it, Martin?'

'That's your problem!'

'Oh no – it's yours, too,' said Bennett, starting to wheel the contraption to the shelter of a hedge.

'You're one of the boys now, Martin,' Stidger said. 'Come on, give me a hand to shove this monster.'

Stormy Passage

All Jimmy Grant knew about Da Silva was what that smooth gentleman chose to tell him. He was, he said, a man who, with three friends, wanted to be landed secretly in their native country, which they had been forced to flee in the course of a revolution.

It was a venture loaded with danger but to Jimmy danger was the spice of life. All the same, he mistrusted Da Silva.

'Then it was agreed we meet at sundown at the place arranged, Señor Grant?' said Da Silva. He was a tall, thin man in a crumpled white suit and with a wide-brimmed sombrero set at a jaunty angle on his dark head.

'It is agreed Señor Da Silva.'

'Here is the first instalment of your fee. The balance will be paid when the mission is completed. *Hasta la vista!*'

Jimmy Grant slid the bulky envelope into the inside pocket of his jacket. He watched Da Silva part the heavy bead curtains draping the entrance to the waterfront cafe and stride out, leaving a trail of cigar smoke swirling behind him.

Jimmy remained where he was, sipping the strong black coffee, more than a little uneasy in his mind lest he had made a big fool of himself.

His launch had been hired in Jamaica by a couple of American scientists to transport them and their equipment to Haiti, where they proposed to make a geological survey of the interior. After he had landed them at Port au Prince, the capital city, and they had gone inland, Jimmy had remained for a few

33

days, taking time off to explore a little of the island.

He took most things as they came, and he had always wanted to visit Haiti. This was the island Columbus called Hispaniola, which became the haunt of French and British buccaneers and, later, the first state to be governed constitutionally entirely by negroes, the descendants of slaves imported to work in the mines and plantations.

All Jimmy knew about Da Silva was what the man had told him. He was, he said, a Guavadan, who, with three companions wanted to be landed secretly in their native country, which they were forced to flee during the course of a revolution. Da Silva had offered him two thousand American dollars, half of which he had just paid him.

It was a venture loaded with danger – but not too difficult for someone who knew the West Indian seas as well as Jimmy did. His launch was fast and seaworthy, built for big sport fishing, well able to cover the distance from Port au Prince to the nearest point on the Guavadan coastline.

Two thousand dollars was a lot of money and Jimmy, to whom danger was the spice of life, had been reluctant to refuse such a tempting offer. All the same, he mistrusted Da Silva. There was something about the man which was furtive and unsatisfactory. But a man who was a refugee from his native country and maybe, in danger of his life, would probably be like that anyway, Jimmy thought. Anyhow, worrying was futile.

He left the cafe and walked along the picturesque waterfront to the jetty at the western end, where he had his launch moored. While most of the island was mountainous and fairly temperate in climate, Port au Prince was built on an alluvial plain and the steaming heat was oppressive, made bearable only by the cooler sea breezes which came in the late afternoon and night.

As he had been expecting to return to Jamaica in the morning he had refuelled and provisioned the launch. All he had to do now was take aboard an extra ten gallons of fuel oil to get him back from Guavada.

When sundown came he was on his way to the cove a mile out of town, which was the rendezvous agreed with Da Silva. When he reached it, he shut off the engine and drifted in until he felt the bow touch sand. He slid over the side, pushed the boat back into deeper water, and dropped anchor.

The sky above him was a dark velvety blue, dotted with twinkling stars, and the heat came off the land in waves. But except for the soft lapping of the sea on the beach it was silent and rather oppressive.

Presently, his sharp ears detected the sound of footsteps coming slowly and cautiously from the dark shadows below the cliffs. Then he saw Da Silva and his companions crossing the sand toward him.

34

Two of them were young and tough. The third was elderly, with a long, thoughtful face and the eyes of a visionary, a gentle looking man, in marked contrast to his companions.

Da Silva helped the old man aboard and sat him aft on the stern seat. He introduced him as Dr Juan Jalvez, and the others as Carlos and Gomez. Jimmy suspected that those might not be their real names, but that was none of his business.

'How long will it take us?' asked Dr Jalvez. He spoke in English with a Southern American accent, a soft quiet voice which somehow matched his appearance.

'With luck, we should sight Guavada by seven or eight o'clock tomorrow morning,' Jimmy told him, and he seemed satisfied.

The long coastline of the peninsula Sierra de Bahouco was studded with reefs and mangrove swamps and Jimmy kept well out to sea as he headed past some islets and met the rolling waves of the Caribbean.

Dr Jalvez, wrapped in a blanket, dozed on the stern seat, but the others kept wide awake, talking softly among themselves. Jimmy took no notice of them, but he was aware that they were restless and, perhaps, apprehensive as to the outcome of the adventure.

It was an hour after dawn when Jimmy sighted the rugged cliffs on the horizon – the most easterly point of Guavada.

He got out his charts again and studied them carefully. His passengers wished to land on a dangerous coast, where ragged-toothed reefs and swiftly flowing currents lay in wait for the unwary navigator.

Jimmy skirted the first of the reefs and felt the launch go momentarily out of control, caught in a tide race. For the next fifteen minutes he battled his way through the hazards until he was in calmer water. He throttled down the engine and moved in cautiously, holding the launch against the heavy drag of a cross tide. Directly inshore lay a small sandy cove, like a narrow cleft in the towering cliffs.

Carlos was already in the dinghy, and Gomez was about to step aboard when suddenly a machine gun opened up from behind the rocks at the cliff base. The bullets swept across the dinghy, dropping Carlos. Gomez cried out in agony and fell back into the launch. Dr Jalvez was about to rise when Jimmy pushed him down again and shouted: 'Stay down.'

Da Silva then swore an oath in Spanish, cursing the hidden gunners. 'Cease fire, you incompetent fools!' he cried angrily. 'Your instructions were to wait until we were ashore!'

In that moment Jimmy realised that it was Da Silva who had betrayed them. With a sudden heave he sent the tall Guavadan overboard, drew his knife, cut the dinghy adrift, and with controlled urgency hauled up the anchor.

Bullets whined viciously around him as he grabbed the wheel and, careless of reefs or tide, opened up full throttle. Twice he felt the ominous lurch as the keel grazed over submerged rock.

Then he was out of the danger zone, racing across open sea, beyond the effective range of the machine guns. He eased the throttle and relaxed, feeling the nervous reaction quivering in his limbs. It had been a close thing and he knew it.

Dr Jalvez crawled up from the bottom boards and slumped upon the stern seat, trembling, his face deathly pale.

'You were betrayed,' said Jimmy. 'Da Silva was responsible. But something must have gone wrong. He was furious when those gunners opened up on us. They should have waited until we were ashore. Carlos was killed. Gomez here is seriously wounded, I'm afraid. You'd better see to him. There's a first aid kit in the cabin.'

'I am a doctor of science, not of medicine,' said Jalvez. 'I am quite useless in dealing with wounds. The sight of blood sickens me.'

Jimmy said nothing as he went down on his knee beside the unconscious Gomez. He saw the ugly rip across his skull, but found no other wounds. It looked as if Gomez had been merely stunned, but there could, of course, be a fracture of the skull. There was nothing that he could do but let him lie quietly until he recovered.

Gomez might be innocent, but on the other hand he might have been working with Da Silva. As a precaution Jimmy slid the .45 Colt revolver from the holster under Gomez's arm, and stuck it in his belt.

'I'm taking you to Jamaica,' he said to Dr Jalvez. 'It is futile to attempt to land now.'

'Thank you,' said the doctor. 'I realise that I have been sadly betrayed by a man I thought was a loyal Guavadan, and my friend.'

Jimmy could have told him that he should have been more careful in the people he accepted as friends. But he was a gentle, unworldly old man and he had suffered enough already. Maybe next time, if there ever was a next time, he would be more critical.

Studying the charts again, Jimmy decided which course he would set, because he did not rule out the possibility that a naval ship might be sent after them.

Fifteen minutes later, as he rounded the long spit of-headland his worst fears were realised. He saw five motor torpedo boats racing toward him in crescent formation. They were similar craft to the E boats once used by the Germans and they carried quad-Oerlikon guns, mounted in small Frazer-Nash turrets. Firing four barrelled they were fearsome weapons at close range. Each boat was armed with two twenty-one inch torpedos, which meant ten in all. Jimmy realised that the odds stacked against him were terrible. His only hope lay in the superior speed of his launch and her stouter frame.

The E boats began to spread out, moving apart like a huge fan opening. The two boats on the ends of the fan suddenly opened cross fire. Jimmy saw the vicious red flashes and heard the shells scream overhead. It was very poor shooting, but maybe they were only intended for warning shots.

He opened up full throttle and drove straight for the gap between the most seaward pair of E boats, who were coming up fast on his port quarter.

The Oerlikons roared in a crazy burst of firing from all the E boats, ploughing up the sea like mighty splashes of rain all around him. A torpedo hissed past his bows at a distance of less than ten feet and he saw the ominous clear against the blue water.

Jimmy began to zig-zag, making thirty degree turns, so that his bows swung first to port, then to starboard, hanging poised for a split second before swinging back once again in the opposite direction. But he quickly realised that his best manoeuvre was the straight dash through the line of boats aiming to encircle him. If he got himself caught in that trap, however bad the gunners might be, they would pound his launch to matchwood.

He was within a couple of hundred metres of the gap, racing at full speed, when the two boats began to swing in, narrowing the gap alarmingly, but he did not attempt to alter course. As the distance rapidly diminished he glimpsed the faces of the Guavadans manning the forward gun and the face of the captain on the tiny bridge of the boat on the port quarter, his mouth open, yelling an order.

At the last fatal moment the E boat swung right across his path. Too late now to swing away. Jimmy momentarily shut his eyes as the steel-bound, knife-edge bow of his launch slashed into the thin casing of the E boat with a grinding crunch of splintered wood and tortured metal. He felt the launch shudder from end to end, check, and then seem to rise out of the water, breaking free triumphantly from her enemy, leaving her to settle beneath the waves.

A moment later Jimmy was steering clear to race across the open sea, away from the trap, with the background din of booming guns and screaming men. He found himself heading towards the shore.

He brought the launch around in a tight, skidding turn of ninety degrees, the engines drumming wildly as the thrashing screws bit into the water sweeping past the hull. As he raced past the fan of E boats he could see the wreckage and the men swimming in the water. But he had no time to feel satisfied. The guns were turned on him again as the E boats swung in line, ready to give chase.

A shell struck the engine cowling, bounced off, but failed to explode on impact. The odds were it had not been properly detonated, or had struck the cowling at an angle and not on the nose cap. Had it exploded it would have blown Jimmy's head off, a fact of which he was all too well aware.

He glanced behind and saw that he was increasing his lead over the E boats. He had the legs of them and with luck would shake them off. The guns were still blazing away, but the shells were falling short. His greatest danger now lay in the possibility that the E boat commander might have called up air assistance and soon he would have dive bombers and machine guns to harrass him.

An hour later the E boats were just black dots on the horizon, turning toward home, having abandoned the chase. Jimmy eased the throttle and sat back, wiping the beads of perspiration from his brow.

For the first time Dr Jalvez spoke as he raised himself painfully from the bottom boards and dropped on the stern seat.

'You are a very brave young man,' he said. 'You have saved my life at great risk to your own.'

Jimmy grinned. 'I don't know about being brave. I was scared stiff when those guns opened up. Fortunately they were rotten shots. You wouldn't have thought they could have missed us, but they did.'

The engine suddenly began to splutter and then died. Jimmy guessed they were out of fuel. He locked the wheel and went forward to where he had the ten gallon drum stowed. As he eased off the cap some of the contents spilled over – and Jimmy knew immediately that something was wrong. There was no odour to the fluid. He dabbed a finger in it and put it to his lips, confirming his suspicions. This was just plain, salt sea water! That crook of a dealer in Haiti had cheated him, probably guessing he was not returning to the island. Jimmy swore softly to himself. He should have checked the contents before he sailed.

Well, it was too late now to moan about his carelessness. All he could do was rig a sail and hope for the best. There was enough water and stores aboard to last four or five days, used with care. But he wasn't at all sure that a sail would be sufficient·to hold the launch against adverse winds and tide.

The launch carried a spare mast and sail for just such an emergency, but Jimmy had never had occasion to use it before. With the help of Dr Jalvez he got the mast fixed and the sail hoisted. If aircraft came over, or the E boats came again he was a sitting duck.

He clamped a tiller on the rudder head and sat back in the stern seat. It was then he observed that Gomez was no longer unconscious, but very much awake, watching him through narrowed lids. He wondered how long he had been like that, pretending. That the man was dangerous, he guessed. But he still had the gun tucked into his belt.

He said, sharply, in Spanish, 'Get up, Gomez! You are not deceiving me.'

Gomez rolled over and sat up. He said, 'Sẽnor, I have no wish to deceive you. I am an honest man – a true friend of the doctor.'

Jimmy glanced at Dr Jalvez. 'How long have you known this man?' he demanded.

'I never saw him before he joined us last night with Da Silva,' declared the doctor. Gomez shrugged, but said nothing.

It was coming sundown when Gomez saw his chance. Jimmy was moving forward to adjust the sail when Gomez whipped out his hand and snatched the revolver from Jimmy's trouser band.

'Head back to Guavada,' he snarled. 'And no tricks.'

Jimmy went back to the tiller and brought the launch around in a tight turn. He would have to wait his opportunity, too.

When darkness fell he said, 'The American fleet patrols this area and Russian submarines have been reported. The Americans will be as nervous as cats in a strange back yard. If they spot us without navigation lights they will run as down and ask questions later.'

To his surprise, Gomez snarled, 'Fix your lights!'

An hour later they were still heading back to Guavada when suddenly a brilliant white beam slashed through the darkness, resting steady on them. Gomez put up a hand to shield his eyes and in that moment Jimmy moved fast, snatching away the revolver.

The long grey shape of an American destroyer materialised behind the searchlight and came alongside the launch. A lieutenant and a C.P.O. slid down a rope ladder and stepped aboard.

'When we saw a boat coming our way with its navigation lights reversed we got curious,' grinned the lieutenant. 'It was a smart way of attracting attention, I guess.' He stared at the doctor and exclaimed, 'Why, it's Dr Jalvez! What a stroke of luck! Who is the other man?'

'A treacherous hound named Gomez,' said Jimmy.

'All right,' said the lieutenant. 'All three of you get aboard the destroyer.'

In the captain's cabin, Jimmy told his story. The captain gave him a hard stare. 'You young fool,' he said, 'Didn't you realise the danger? Dr Jalvez is the president of the exiled Guavadans in the United States. He was being lured back to Guavada by secret agents of the revolutionary government, who would certainly have executed him. Well, there's a ten thousand dollar reward for the person who rescues him. I guess you qualify for it! But don't be such a venturesome mug again. You can't always have such fool's luck. We're going to Jamaica ourselves, so you had better stay aboard. Your launch can be towed. Does that satisfy you?'

'It does, sir. I'm much obliged to you.'

The captain smacked a friendly hand on Jimmy's shoulder. 'It's we who should be obliged to you, son. You saved the life of a fine old man who might one day restore liberty to his countrymen. Maybe you weren't so crazy after all.'

The Ruby of Kalu

For some hours the glass had been falling and the hands aboard the brig Celebes Star *set to work shortening sail in preparation for the storm that was bound to follow. But storms in the China Sea have a habit of blowing up swiftly and young Dick and his veteran shipmate Ben Wagstaff were caught aloft by the sudden squall.*

Before they could reach the deck, the rest of the crew had abandoned ship, for already the Celebes Star *had struck an unseen reef.*

Dick and Ben were alone aboard a holed ship!

Old Ben Wagstaff was whittling away at a piece of wood, fashioning a tiny ship model. Idly, I watched his deft movements with the knife, as he began to carve the name on the hull of the model.

'What name will you give her, Ben?' I asked, breaking a ten minutes' silence.

Ben grunted. 'Reckon I'll name her the *Ruby*,' he answered.

'What makes you say that, Ben?'

Ben gave a final touch to a letter and faced me. ''Cause I like rubies. Want to see some?' He reached inside his seaman's jersey and produced a small wash-leather bag which hung round his neck on a thong. He undid the draw-string, and poured out five tiny red stones into his hand.

I gave an exclamation and stared at the stones. 'Are they rubies, Ben?' I asked. 'Real rubies?'

Ben nodded. 'Aye, they're real enough. But they're small. Though I

41

reckon I'll make a fairish profit back in Portsmouth.'

Ben poured the tiny gems into my hand, and the tropical sun shot red fire into them. 'They're fine,' I said, admiringly.

'But small,' Ben went on. 'Very small. Why, I've seen rubies ten times this size. Ever heard of the Ruby of Kalu?'

I shook my head. 'Never. Was that a big stone?'

Ben was about to reply, when a shout came from the bosun, calling all hands to shorten sail, and we both had to dash forward. Our brig, the *Celebes Star,* was somewhere in the South China sea, and for some hours the glass had been falling. Even as the hands set to work shortening sail, the sun disappeared into a bank of leaden cloud.

I wasn't a bad seaman, although the only experience I'd had was with the native boys of Singapore, when we'd taken out small craft into the Straits. I'd been brought up in the Colony, although I was born in Dorset. My father had bought a plantation in the Straits Settlements which had prospered for many years. Then, we had a disastrous crop failure, and an epidemic of cholera.

Somehow, I escaped the disease; perhaps because I'd lived a hardy life, running wild with the native lads. Grief-stricken, I watched first my mother, and then my father, die. The plantation was neglected and rapidly fell into decay, and before long I was penniless.

The only person of influence I knew in Singapore was a Eurasian named Peters who worked near the harbour. He knew some of the shipping people, and it was he who managed to get me signed aboard the *Celebes Star* as an ordinary seaman.

The brig was bound for Shanghai from London, with machinery and Birmingham ware. Although I had signed for the return trip to London, I knew it would be many months before I sighted England again.

I was up in the crosstrees with old Ben, and even as we climbed the ratlines, the squall hit us. Wind and water struck the brig like a massive blow from the hand of a giant. All the breath was knocked from my body, and I gripped the ratline stuff with all my strength. For many hours, it seemed (although really it was only about twenty minutes), we clung there, like flies caught in a giant spider's web. Then, as the squall died down, I glanced up towards the motionless figure of Ben, clinging to the ropes.

When at last it seemed safe to move, I began to climb down, and Ben called: 'All right, Dick?'

I was about to answer 'Yes', when a violent shock jarred the whole ship, and I was almost torn from my hold. Ben was still above me, and I heard his voice, filled with horror.

'We've struck! By thunder, Dick, we've struck!'

As he spoke, there came another rending crash, followed by shouts of terror from the crew below. Then, all was confusion. Officers were giving orders, men were shouting, and above it all came a sickening, grinding sound, as the hull of the brig battered itself to pieces on an unseen reef.

Suddenly, came another shout:

'Abandon ship! Abandon ship!'

With a thrill of horror, I realised that Ben and I must hurry to reach the deck. We both swung down the ratlines, dodging the falling tackle, and desperate with fear. Miraculously, we reached the deck, which was canted at a steep angle.

The sea was whipped into fresh fury, and crashed up and over the deck, carrying loose lumber with it. It was impossible to stand upright on the deck, and we had to climb along, clinging to any handhold available. At last, I fetched up against a capstan, and Ben crawled up beside me.

Then, suddenly, the squall passed. The seas died down and the sky grew lighter. As the sun broke through, I stretched my aching limbs, and worked my fingers, white and numbed with long immersion in salt water.

Ben had crawled up to a deck housing which now stood out crazily at an angle above our heads. Then seating himself upon it, he called to me to follow him up.

'Reckon we're the only ones left aboard, Dick, lad. Others took off in the boats, but I don't give much for their chances of gettin' through alive.' He began feeling in his pockets for his tobacco.

'That squall would have capsized the small boats,' I agreed.

'Aye,' Ben nodded, finding his twist of black tobacco. Biting off a piece, he chewed and added, 'These are treacherous seas.'

I settled myself down on the side of the deck housing. 'We'd best take a look over the ship,' I suggested. 'Maybe one of the boats . . .'

I broke off, as, with a thrill of surprise, I realised that somewhere aboard the stricken brig a voice was calling.

'By Jiminy, Dick!' said old Ben. 'Did ye hear that?'

I nodded. 'Came from down below. Come on, Ben!'

We clambered across the tangle of ropes and wreckage, and made our way towards the open hatchway which gave into the hold. From out of the inky depths, we could hear a voice, calling faintly.

Ben called down into the hold. 'Ahoy! Who's there?'

Immediately the voice replied, slightly louder.

'Can't see a blamed thing,' said Ben. 'Dick, lad, I've a mind there's a lantern hanging in the wheelhouse. It's well protected with wire and such. There's matches besides, in a box in the bulkhead store there. It'll be locked, but you can smash it open with the axe which is there in a rack beside. Hurry and bring the lantern here. And find a length of line.'

I hurried off as best I could, and found the lantern, as Ben said, intact, except that it had jammed against a timber in the roof. I found the axe and removed it from its housing; with a light blow from its handle, I released the lantern, and then broke open the locker in the bulkhead. Sure enough, there were matches inside, and I managed to light the lantern. There was plenty of tangled line about, and I chose a piece which looked least tangled, cutting it out with my knife.

Ben, still looking down into the hold, grasped the lantern. 'Good boy, Dick. Now, we'll just bend the line to the lantern handle, and lower it down into the hold.'

Suiting his action to the word, he let down the line, and the flickering light gave a dim kind of illumination in the blackness. Then, we saw him, a dark, slight figure, clinging desperately to a large cask which floated in the flooded hold.

'I'll need a rope, Ben. You'll have to let me down and we'll haul him out.' As Ben nodded, I scrambled away, and returned a short while later with a coil of rope.

'Now, do you listen to me, Dick,' said Ben. 'I'll take the rope around yonder capstan. I see there's a couple of timber levers still there. Then, we'll lower you down, with a harness hitch on the end of the rope. Then, you'll have to take hold of the poor fellow, and slip him into the rope.'

I nodded. 'Aye, aye, Ben. I'll holler as soon as I've got him all nice and trim.'

Before long, we had him on deck, where he lay against the port rail, quite exhausted, and seemingly half-dead. He was a native boy, scarcely more than fourteen or so, and his only clothing was a tattered shirt and a dirty pair of calico trousers. There was very little we could do for him, and as the sun was now quite warm, we let him lie where he was.

I noticed that Ben was looking somewhat anxious. 'What is it, Ben?' I asked him.

'We're settlin', lad,' he said at last. 'Reckon the old *Star* ain't got more'n a few hours left in her. Then she'll be in Davy Jones's Locker.'

I realised that we must move quickly. 'The boats have all gone, Ben,' I said. 'We'll have to make a raft of some sort.'

Ben nodded. 'Aye. I was thinking of yon hatch cover.' He pointed a stubby brown finger towards a large object which was lying by the stump of a mast. 'If we could shift it down, I reckon it would slide right into the water,' he said.

The hatch-cover was jammed against the mast-stump, caught up with broken rigging. Ben went up and began cutting away at the ropes and cables, and when the hatch-cover was almost clear, he yelled down to me.

'Fetch the rope, Dick. But leave it fast to the capstan.'

I knew what he wanted to do. When the hatch-cover entered the water, Ben wanted to make sure it didn't float away, so he was going to make it fast to a rope first.

Ben finished cutting away at the tangle of ropes which held the hatch-cover, and it began to slide, faster and faster, until it hit the water with a splash.

'Best leave it there, for now,' Ben said. 'It'll be fast enough.'

'All right, Ben,' I said. 'Perhaps we can talk to our boy now. See, he's coming round.'

The small, dusky figure had begun to stir, and now he lifted his head and stared towards us. I went across to him and made to help him up.

He smiled as he gripped the rail. 'You – English?' he asked.

I nodded. 'Yes. Are you all right?'

He looked puzzled, and then I guessed that he had but the merest glimmering of the English tongue. I repeated myself, this time in Malay. At once, his face lit up, and he replied, but his accent was a little strange. We talked for a few minutes, and he explained that he was a Thai, from somewhere up near the Burmese border.

Meanwhile, Ben was getting stores ready to put aboard the raft, and the boy and I gave him a hand with the loading. We found a large water breaker almost full, which we managed to move and set on the raft. At last, after several hours' work, all was safely lashed down, and we clambered aboard the raft ourselves. The old *Star* was now much lower in the water, and it was obvious that she could not last more than an hour.

Ben had rigged a mast, and had found a piece of sail, while an oar would serve as a rudder. Not that we expected to be able to navigate the ungainly craft properly, but we expected to be able to sail her towards the mainland of Indo-China, which was the best part of four hundred miles away.

All signs of bad weather had disappeared, and now the sun blazed strongly from a cloudless sky. There was a mild breeze, which sent our craft moving along at a speed of several knots. We spent some time in rigging a shelter from pieces of spar and sail, for there was almost no shade.

We took a rest at last, and I noticed Ben examining his belt pouch and the wash-leather bag which still hung from his neck. I remembered his rubies and asked if they were safe?

'Aye,' Ben nodded. 'They're safe, but I only thank God we're safe ourselves.'

The Siamese boy was sitting watching as Ben filled his pipe. He was a fine looking fellow, with a kind of aristocratic poise about him. He told me very little about himself, except that his name was U Fan.

It had puzzled me at first when we had discovered him down in the hold. I couldn't remember him as a member of the crew, but Ben told me that the boy had been picked up by the *Celebes Star* one night, from a small boat.

No one was quite certain what had happened, but the Captain was satisfied that the boy had been aboard a local craft which had been attacked by Malay pirates. It had not been established how he had got away, for the pirates were quite ruthless, and rarely allowed anyone to escape alive.

Ben's voice broke in upon my thoughts.

'I never did get to telling you about that marvellous ruby, Dick, did I?' he rumbled.

'Eh?' I said, bringing myself back to earth. 'The ruby? Oh yes, Ben. You were going to spin a yarn about this big stone – what was it called?'

Ben gave a puff on his pipe. 'The Ruby of Kalu.'

As he spoke, the Siamese boy sat bolt upright. 'Kalu!' he said, 'Kalu!'

'You know about it?' I asked. 'You know about the famous ruby?' I forgot to speak in Malay, and had to repeat it again in that language.

U Fan nodded, excitedly. He explained that he knew the ruby well but was surprised that an English seaman should know of its wonders. I asked him to explain more, but he would only say that it was a great source of wonder, and we had to be content with that.

I suppose I should tell in detail of our long trip across the China Sea on that raft; of how we became weary of exhaustion and almost burnt black with the tropical sun, but the memory of the journey is still too painful for me to dwell upon it. Suffice to say, after two weeks, we were spotted by a barque off the Kondor Islands, and within days were safe ashore at Saigon.

We were all three well looked after in a hospital there, run by the French, and a week later, were well enough to be discharged. There was a small matter of payment to be considered, but apart from Ben's rubies, we were without funds. So poor Ben had to sell his rubies. He got a decent price for them, I think.

But U Fan hadn't forgotten our interest in the Ruby of Kalu. He still wouldn't tell us much about it, but explained that if we were to visit the fabulous place where it was kept, all would go well for us. For myself, I was inclined to forget it, and make our way to an English port and then home, but Ben was greatly intrigued and full of the strange notions which seemed to fill sailormen's heads.

After much discussion, with myself interpreting, Ben decided he would go with U Fan to see the Ruby, and was most insistent on my going too. Poor old Ben had used his rubies to help us out of a hole, and I felt it only right to do as he wished.

So we got ourselves new outfits, and started on the long journey to the place U Fan had mentioned. This meant a sea voyage once again from Saigon to Bangkok, which was accomplished in a French steamer. From Bangkok we went up-river through hundreds of miles, up into the hills of the north.

The river wound through dense forests of green, tropical trees hung with vines. The air was filled with the screeches of brilliantly coloured birds and the scuttling forms of dozens of small animals. Then we left the forest behind, and came out on to a plain, with crowded villages cluttering the river banks.

Once in the hills, the river dwindled, and at last we had to quit our boats and move along on foot. Leaving the boatmen far behind, the three of us went on alone, moving from the foothills into the mountains. Days went by, then weeks. Now we were high up in the mountains, somewhere between Siam, Burma and Indo-China. We may have been into China itself, for we had no maps.

Then, at last, we came to his village. There was no doubt that it was U Fan's village, for he was recognised immediately. People rushed up to him and embraced him, and soon, we had a crowd accompanying us through the place.

Most of the buildings were small and unremarkable, but we realised that U Fan was something of a local celebrity, for his house was by far the most handsome of all. Then we discovered that he was the son of the chief.

Exactly what his rank was, we never knew but U Fan's father was undoubtedly a very important man, and apparently well off. When he saw his son, he burst into tears, and was completely overcome.

Ben looked quite embarrassed. 'Perhaps we'd best leave them to it, Dick, my lad,' he said. We made to move off, but U Fan stopped us, explaining that while we were in the village, we must be his guests.

So Ben and I were given two very comfortable beds in a room at the front of the house. Later, we were invited to supper with the chief, his son, and the rest of the family, of whom there seemed to be about twenty. There was much gaiety, and song-singing until quite late, so that Ben and I were glad to get to bed.

We slept well, and next morning U Fan called us to breakfast, explaining that we were to be taken to Kalu, where we should see the fabulous Ruby. After breakfast, a small procession formed up, and we all set off towards the end of the village, where there lay a large lake. Here we stopped, and U Fan pointed towards the centre of the lake where a tiny islet lay, in the very centre of which there stood a squat pagoda-like building, surrounded by green trees.

'Him Kalu,' U Fan said, making one of his very rare English speeches. Several boats were got ready, and oarsmen sculled us across the lake towards the islet. Ten minutes later, we were standing on a landing stage of white stone, and U Fan led us towards the pagoda. As we walked, U Fan talked to me in Malay.

'This building is a temple,' he explained. 'Kalu is a spirit – the spirit of all our ancestors – the embodiment of life itself. Here we come each holy day to make our offering to the spirit of Kalu. In this place, our ancestors have come for centuries to give what they could to Kalu. My father, as the prince, will make a good offering, but the poor peasant will only be able to give something small, perhaps a piece of carving made by himself.'

Two priests drew open the carved doors of the pagoda, and we entered into the circular chamber within.

At first, it was difficult to see, for the light, which came from above, was red – deep red. As our eyes became accustomed to the red light, we could see that the whole of the chamber was filled with objects of all kinds. There were beautifully carved elephants of jade and ivory, magnificent carved ornaments of gold and silver, magnificent gems fashioned into necklaces, combs and clasps, dishes filled with coins of gold and silver, and hundreds of caskets, each containing a special treasure of its own. From all sides the red light flashed on sparkling jewels, and mixed up with them all stood the humbler offerings: inlaid boxes, strands of hair woven into fantastic designs, and even offerings made simply from straw.

As we looked, U Fan pointed upwards, towards the source of the red light. 'See,' he said, 'the Ruby of Kalu.'

Ben and I looked up, and gasped. There, at the apex of the chamber, was a great red stone, larger in size even than an ostrich's egg. It was an enormous gem, perhaps of five or six thousand carats, and would have been worth a king's ransom.

U Fan went on speaking to me in Malay. 'Now, Kalu repays her debt,' he said, and handed me a casket of carved ivory. 'For my two English deliverers,' he said. As he spoke, he turned, and made his way out of the temple.

Six months passed before we reached England again, so Ben and I had plenty of time to discuss our future. By the time we actually docked in London, we'd made our plans.

Now, as I write from my study on the Dorset coast, I can see old Ben making his way towards the cliffs overlooking the beach. Ben decided to 'swallow the anchor', and settle down within sight and sound of the sea.

For myself, there's the farm, with a good herd of Jerseys, and several acres of good wheatland. For me, too, there's the sea, for I could never go too far away from it. Despite its wild fury, the sea can be gentle, and once it's in your blood, you'll never be rid of it.

Kalu's gift, by the way, was worth a great deal of money. The casket contained some white stones, considered by the people of U Fan's village to be of much lesser value than the beautiful red rubies. But Ben and I didn't mind, as the white stones turned out to be diamonds!

Hotside

Nick Douglas had quarrelled bitterly with his brother Clive . . . had broken with him completely. But now his brother with two other men was down beyond the Twilight Zone, trapped in a wrecked ship.

Someone had to reach that disabled space-craft before the tremendous heat broke down the ship's refrigeration plant.

But a saboteur was determined that, come what may, Nick Douglas would never save his brother.

Nick Douglas turned away from the harsh glare beyond the tinted observatory window as his assistant entered the room.

Ron Buckley's expression was that of a cat who had got at the cream as he said; 'There's news about the ship.' He licked his lips. 'Bad news, Nick.'

Nick Douglas, meteorologist at the sun observatory on Mercury wondered: *'Bad for whom?'* Not for Buckley, judging by his expression. . . . And his mind flashed back to the day Buckley had told him of the ship bringing his brother to Mercury. Buckley hadn't liked that, because Clive Douglas was going to replace him in his post.

Buckley had been sure it was Nick's idea. He didn't know how things stood between Nick and his brother; didn't know of the row they'd had, the break between them.

'Well, what's happened?' Nick demanded, lifting his voice above the hum of the computers.

'The ship's down – crashed on Hotside!'

Nick heard the words as if they came from far away, through a waterfall of sound. His head turned to the window, and the glare of Mercury's permanently illuminated sun-side struck him like a physical blow. 'Out there?'

He grasped Buckley's shoulders and shook him roughly. 'This isn't some kind of a gag you've dreamed up?'

'It just came through on the radio,' Buckley said, sullen. 'I thought I'd tell you myself.'

Nick looked at him with distaste, shocked by the realisation that this meant nothing to Buckley except that a potential rival had been eliminated. It became suddenly urgent to get him to see this in the right perspective.

'Forget Clive, and your job. There's a two-man crew aboard the *British Lion* – they're in danger, too! Doesn't that mean anything to you?'

Nick thought: '*Three men down beyond the Twilight Zone, trapped in a wrecked ship. . . .*'

'There's nothing we can do,' Buckley said suddenly. 'I mean, it's all over, isn't it?'

Clive! Nick could still remember their last quarrel, felt the same surge of anger – but he knew he had to try to save his brother. Had to. Blood was thicker than water.

'No, by glory, it's not all over!' He whirled from the observatory to the radio room. 'Give me the details.'

Jim Reeves looked up from his set. 'A mess, Nick. There's no chance of repairing the *Lion*. Refrigeration's still okay though – Captain Franklin reckons they can last out forty-eight hours.'

Nick thought furiously. Forty-eight hours – he had to perform a miracle in that time. 'What's her position?'

'Almost due east – about thirty miles past the edge of the Twilight Zone.'

Thirty miles across Hotside – and he had to rescue them. *How*? Men had died trying to make that crossing; no one had ever succeeded.

'Start calling for help, Jim. Maybe there's another ship close enough to rescue them in time.'

Time was the important factor. Mercury was the closest planet to the Sun, a mere thirty-six million miles away, compared to Earth's ninety-three. Someone had to reach them before the tremendous heat broke down their refrigeration plant. When that happened, the end would come quickly.

Nick returned to the observatory. There must be something he could do . . . .

He had forgotten his assistant, till Buckley said: 'Forget it, Nick – there's nothing you can do.'

'We've got to try –.'

Buckley pointed, dramatically, to the view beyond the tinted window. Automatically, Nick's gaze went out across the Twilight Zone. This was the only habitable area for men – between the freezing cold of the dark side of the planet and the permanently illuminated hemisphere. A ball of fire was hanging huge and low in the sky.

'Rescue them? Out there?' Mockery filled Buckley's voice. 'Now I know you're mad! No-one can live in that furnace. It's impossible to reach them, and you know it. We've no ship here, and by surface it's . . . it's just miles and miles of red-hot lava beds and molten metal!' His voice dropped to a whisper. 'Don't even think about it, Nick. It's certain death out there.'

'Certain death for three men, unless we come up with an idea!'

'Give it up, Nick! Lay off the heroics. Let's face it, you'll be wasting your life as well as your time if you go out –.'

Nick glared at his assistant. 'Shut up!'

By surface, he thought; there was the Cat – a refrigerated cabin mounted on caterpillar treads – but it had been designed only to approach the edge of Hotside. Could it stand the trip, and return? And it was so slow . . . then he remembered the Cat was stripped down for main-tenance.

'Understand this, Buckley, we've got to try. Got to. There's Franklin and Tausky, as well as my brother.'

Buckley said nothing. Looking at him, Nick guessed his thoughts: *Save Clive, and he, Buckley, lost his job.* Angry, Nick turned and went to the door, shouted down to the workshop: 'Michaels! Get the Cat ready, fast – we're going out!'

But he wondered: would they really be able to do anything? He imagined the *Lion,* lying disabled on that scorched surface under a flaming sun, and shuddered.

A shout from Reeves roused him: 'Franklin's on the air!'

Nick ran to the radio room. Static crackled from a wall speaker, almost drowning out Franklin's voice as Nick grabbed for the mike.

'Hullo, captain – Douglas here. We're readying a party to come and get you. How are things now? Is my brother all right?'

Franklin's reply was faint, and he had to strain to catch the words:

'. . . Bad, Nick . . . brother's okay, but the fridge is cracking under the overload . . . wasn't built for this sort of treatment.'

Nick started to sweat. The refrigeration plant cracking; it must be ghastly out there. 'How long can you hold on?'

Reeves adjusted a dial as static from the sun's flares carried off Franklin's voice.

'. . . Reckon twelve hours at most . . . heat's building up all the time . . . any hope . . . .'

Twelve hours! Nick was stunned. No-one could possibly do anything in that time. He imagined the *Lion's* interior, the temperature soaring and the air drying out, clothing discarded and bodies sweating.

'Yeah,' he said gruffly. 'Don't give up hope – we'll get to you. Just stick it out.'

He glanced round and saw Buckley leaning against the door of the radio room, and knew what he was thinking. In just twelve hours, his job was safe. He didn't seem to visualise what it meant to the trapped men; death on Hotside was the ultimate in horror.

On Hotside, the temperature went up to seven hundred degrees, and there were pools of molten metal to cross. There wasn't a chance, Nick thought wearily, but still he had to try. He moistened his lips and spoke into the microphone again: 'We'll get you out, captain – somehow!'

He left the radio room and went down to the workshop. 'Michaels – there's no time for anything elaborate now. Just get the Cat working. We've got to leave in a hurry!'

He worked with Michaels and his engineers, sweating it out to ready the Cat for the trip. Even if they reassembled it in reasonable time, he would not feel optimistic. The Cat was a slow-moving vehicle.

He drove the engineers hard. Speed was the only thing that could give those aboard the *Lion* any chance at all.

Then Reeves came in. 'There's only one ship anywhere near, Nick, and they say they can't make it in less than fifteen hours.'

Nick nodded grimly. He'd been praying a ship was close enough to save this impossible overland trip. Three hours too late . . . it had to be the Cat now.

'All right,' he shouted at the engineers, 'you heard the man! What are you waiting for? Let's get this job finished – we're going to do it the hard way!'

He thought of Clive as he tightened a nut. It was up to him. The trip would be bad; he'd touched the edge of Hotside more than once when he'd been replacing damaged instruments at the remote testing sites – now he had to enter it. He tried to anticipate all the things that could go wrong, to give himself the best chance of success.

Where had those others failed who had died trying to cross Hotside?

As he worked, the minutes dragged by and piled up into seemingly endless hours for Nick.

There was no real chance, he told himself, but he was going through with it. All the way. He felt he had no alternative, for Clive dominated his thoughts as the Sun dominated that inferno just over the horizon.

He would go himself, because he dare not trust anyone else to push the Cat to its limit of endurance. He would go alone. The tiny cabin held three in comfort, four at a squash; there was simply no room for anyone else.

'Ready in fifteen minutes,' Michaels announced.

Nick nodded and hurried back to the radio-room. He stopped short in the doorway as a familiar voice – *Clive's* voice – came over the speaker: 'Nick – Nick Douglas . . . can you hear me . . . ?'

He grabbed the mike. 'I hear you, Clive.'

'Nick, it's no good.' Clive's voice sounded hoarse, despairing. 'The heat . . . it's stifling . . . there isn't time now – don't take the risk . . . .'

Static faded out some of his words.

'Patch things up between us . . . it wasn't your fault, Nick. . . .'

Nick gripped the microphone tighter, his hand sweating, trying to keep his hopelessness out of his voice. 'Listen, Clive, hold on. I'm starting in the next fifteen minutes. Just hold on!'

'Too late . . . we're being cooked alive . . . .'

Nick was vaguely aware of Buckley standing in the doorway, watching him. 'The Cat's nearly ready to roll. Hang on!' He put down the mike, one thought beating through him like a pulse: he had to save his brother.

He looked round and saw that Buckley had vanished. Michaels stood there. 'Waiting for you, Nick.'

Nick nodded, and walked blindly past him. If he failed, death in twelve hours. Less than that now. He stumbled going down the stairs. So many things could go wrong. His legs carried him faster, faster . . . get moving, he thought, get the Cat out. Then he heard the sound of a hammer, the clatter of metal.

He flung open the workshop door and stared in. A figure crouched in the shadow by the Cat, hammer in hand, pounding furiously.

'What the devil? *Buckley!* What in heaven's name are you up to?'

Nick darted forward as Buckley gave a final smashing blow with a sledge-hammer. A cotter pin flew out, and one of the caterpillar tracks crashed to the floor like a gigantic metal snake.

Nick froze in shock. Then he grabbed Buckley and snatched the hammer from his hand. 'Get out! Get out of here – don't you realise what you've done?

Franklin and Tausky's lives, as well as my brother's, hang on this machine, and you – you – .'

He couldn't find words to describe Buckley. He turned away, disgusted, as his contemptible assistant raved: 'Your brother! Why should I lose my job because of him? I don't care what you think. I'd do anything to stop you!'

Nick's hand clenched. He almost hit Buckley; then his hand dropped to his side in despair. Time! He'd lost more time . . . .

Buckley said, eagerly: 'I'm really saving your life, Nick, don't you see that? If you try to cross Hotside, you'll die, too.' His voice was unnaturally shrill.

'Get away from me,' Nick said curtly, and shouted for Michaels. As he stooped to inspect the track, he thought: how long will this take to replace?

This was the end. He must be too late now. He stood looking down at the track . . . *the track!*

Nick Douglas kept his gaze steady on the horizon as the Cat raced across Hotside.

Mercury was a planet that always had the same side towards the sun, as the moon does to Earth. The side facing away was dark as night and cold as outer space. Only in the narrow Twilight Zone could men live.

He left the observatory and the Twilight Zone far behind him. Through the tinted cabin window he saw the immense shadows thrown across a bone-white surface by a distant line of jagged mountains. From time to time, the red flare of a volcanic upheaval showed great chasms in the scorched rock. He saw sluggish rivers of molten metal. And, over it all, hung the blazing ball of the sun . . . this was Hotside!

He sweated continuously in his asbestos suit even with the cabin refrigerator going full blast. The level of the thermometer rose and rose, reminding him how bad it must be for the three men in the *Lion*.

Coming, Clive, I'm coming. . . .

He had only the crudest control over the Cat now, and it gave him a rough ride. But what the heck? Speed was the main thing, and he had plenty of that. His new rig had increased the Cat's speed ten-fold . . . .

If Buckley hadn't removed a track, he would never have thought of the idea at all. It had been a mad hour's work to remove the other caterpillar track, mount the cabin on runners and lash rocket tubes in place. For fuel he had cylinders of liquid oxygen.

His rocket-powered sled skimmed Mercury's half-molten surface like a crazy thing! He swerved to avoid a crevasse, for he could not afford to be careless at the speed he was moving.

His eyes ached from staring out across the bleached surface into the reflected glare of the sun, searching for the wrecked ship somewhere ahead of him. A vast silence hung over a world of pumice dust and lava beds, torrid light pouring down from that huge ball of fire in the sky.

He rocketed on, mile after mile over hazardous terrain, calculating speed against time. There was a chance now. The sled skimmed along, rockets blazing.

Then he saw a glittering metal cone shape ahead, jutting from the barren landscape. The *Lion*! Praying he was in time. Nick arrowed for the ship and cut his rockets as he approached.

He stopped, waiting. A circular airlock swung open with tantalising slowness and three asbestos-suited figures stumbled out under the fiery blast.

They crossed the short gap and came in through the cabin lock, one at a time, crammed sardine-like inside. Clive removed his helmet and gloves, smiling, and held out his hand.

Nick Douglas gripped his brother's hand; then thumbed the rocket-firing button and headed back for the observatory in the Twilight Zone.

The Vanished Wreck

The steamer Lexton *had foundered off the Irish coast only a few weeks ago and young Skipper Kaye, who had taken on the contract to salvage the* Lexton's *cargo of motor cars, reckoned the task would be a fairly straightforward job.*

Down into the gloomy depths of the sea went Kaye to the last resting place of the sunken ship. He looked round, expecting to see the rusted iron of the ship. To his profound astonishment the wreck had gone!

'Right, Shamus,' grinned Skipper Kaye, the young captain of the schooner *Dolphin*. 'Get going with that Spanner. Bolt me in.'

He took a last breath of fresh air before the spanner grated on the nuts that closed the face-piece of the weird diving helmet he wore.

The helmet had started life as the pressure dome of a railway engine and Shamus had picked it up in a scrap yard. From the same place had come the strange array of gadgets, including a small propeller, which bristled from Kaye's head. There were parts of a sewing machine there, parts of a motor car, parts of farm machinery, all linked by a complicated mass of pipes and cables so that the young skipper looked like a walking Inventor's Club.

Shamus Kelly, engineer of the *Dolphin,* gave a last turn to the last bolt. Skipper Kaye turned to the side and clambered heavily down the ladder there and into the cold, rolling waters of the Irish Sea. A moment later and he was gone.

'Faith, I hope the suit works all right,' breathed Kelly as he watched the bubbles rising where his young captain had vanished.

'This is a fine time to start hoping,' growled Abdullah, the huge negro who was Mate of the *Dolphin*. 'Mistah Kelly . . . I warn you . . . it had better work.'

'And why wouldn't it?' demanded the red-headed Irishman. 'Didn't I make it with me own two hands that have as much skill in them as a whole factory ashore?'

Yet the anxiety did not fade from his eyes as he gazed downward. Now that his young captain was actually using the suit he had a half wish that he had never made it. It had been tested before, of course, but never in such deep water, never with so much at stake. And if he had not made it, Kaye would never have taken on this job . . .

A rusty iron buoy rolled in the water a ship's length away, a wreck buoy, marking the last resting place of the steamer *Lexton* which had foundered off the Irish coast a few weeks before. Skipper Kaye had taken on the contract to salvage the *Lexton's* cargo of motor cars, a contract which could bring in some much-needed money to the *Dolphin*.

Now the young skipper had reached the bottom, which was mud. He peered around for the shape of the wrecked ship.

In the gloom of the sea bottom, he could see little. His hand went to the helmet and pressed a switch. A dazzling beam of light shot out from the built-in lamp.

'Should be over that way,' Kaye told himself after a glance at the compass on his wrist.

In the water he weighed almost nothing and with every step he rose high from the sea floor, moving forward only slowly. Again his hand went to the helmet.

'That's better,' he grinned.

The little propeller on the helmet was now whirling round, driving him forward. The propeller was turned by the air that he had already used so that the rate of his own breathing determined his speed.

Smoothly Kaye glided forward across the sea bottom, disturbing a shoal of whiting, sending them flashing off into the darkness. A big skate went flapping away like some monstrous underwater bird.

For some minutes Kaye glided on, his eye on his wrist compass to make sure he was on the right track. Still he had not reached the wreck though he should have found it long before. Was his compass not pointing truly?

The young skipper began to circle. Into the white beam of his lamp there came something thick and straight and knobbly. He recognised it at once as the cable of the wreck buoy.

Switching off the propeller, he gripped the buoy and pulled himself downward. In a few moments his feet should be resting on the deck of the sunken *Lexton*.

Down he went the last few feet. Then there was something solid under him. He looked around, expecting to see the rusted iron of the ship.

But there was nothing there!

Beneath his feet there was only the concrete mooring block of the buoy! Around him there was but the empty mud of the sea bottom.

Somehow, the wreck had gone!

Sea-Bed Search

For long moments the young skipper could not believe the evidence of his eyes. The buoy mooring still here, yet the wreck had vanished.

'It can't have shifted,' he muttered into his helmet. 'It just can't.'

With the buoy as centre he began to swim out in wider and wider circles.

Still there was no sign of the missing wreck. Baffled, the young skipper headed for the surface where his crew greeted him with relief.

Ah Lee, the Chinese cook, had a big pot of tea already waiting and all three crowded round eagerly to hear just what the task of salvage was going to involve.

Their astonishment was as great as Kaye's when he told them he had not been able to find the ship.

'Skippah,' rumbled Abdullah, 'it looks like that buoy has shifted.'

'With a two hundredweight sinker?' Kaye answered. 'Not a hope. That sinker would hold a ship against a gale let along a buoy – and there haven't been any gales since the *Lexton* went down.'

It seemed that there could be only one explanation. The wreck buoy had somehow been dropped in the wrong spot. With his sextant the young skipper got an exact 'fix' from the sun. As he marked it down on the chart, he was more puzzled than ever. The wreck buoy was on the exact spot that the captain of the *Lexton* had given as his sinking. The buoy was in place all right. Only one answer was left. Unlikely though it seemed, the wreck must have shifted.

'There must be a powerful current down there,' Kaye told his shipmates. 'Though I can't say I noticed it. It's the only answer . . . a current powerful enough to shift a ship.'

Downcast, his crew gazed at him.

'Then the job's over,' sighed Kelly. 'Faith and I was looking forward to the work. It was going to be tricky and I had some new gadgets all worked out to get the cargo up.'

'Who said the job's over?' Kaye retorted. 'We've got a contract – and we're going to carry it out, by thunder. The snag is that now we have to find our wreck first.'

There was only one way to do that. They dropped an anchor at one end of a mile-long cable and sailed the ship in a circle round it so that the cable was sweeping the sea bottom. When it reached the wreck, the cable would be held and would lead them to the wreck's position.

It was a long, slow task. As soon as one area was swept and discovered empty of the wreck they had to lift the anchor and move on. And there were endless delays when the cable snagged a rock to raise their hopes, hopes that vanished as soon as Kaye went down to investigate. Days passed and still they had not found the missing wreck.

They were still searching when a representative of the insurance company which would be paying the salvage money came out to the schooner in a motor boat. He was not impressed by the *Dolphin,* now mudstained by the constant heaving of the sweeps. With Kaye he was very short.

'You've got to do better than this,' he rapped. 'In another month the bad weather will be on us. That will mean stopping operations over the winter. By next spring the cargo will not be worth salving. It's grease-packed but that will save it for only a few weeks. If you can't get results we'll have to find someone who can.'

Kaye tried to point out that the wreck was not in the place he had been told, but his objections were brushed aside. Grimly he watched the insurance launch pull away. Then he called his crew together.

'We've got to find that wreck,' he rapped, 'if we have to work night and day. We can't afford to lose this contract.'

While the sweeping went on, he was scanning his chart, trying to puzzle out how the current could have carried away the wreck, where it could have carried it to. The baffling thing about it was that there were no currents marked on the chart.

Was it possible that the *Lexton's* captain had made a mistake in his position at the time of the sinking? In the panic of abandoning ship a man could easily blunder. Yet his position had been fixed, too, by shore radio stations which had caught the *Lexton's* SOS.

For another night and day the schooner swept the sea bottom. The crew slept only in snatches, rising at every call that the cable was fast. Disappointment after disappointment followed.

'Faith,' sighed Kelly. 'I'd never have believed there were so many rocks anywhere.'

Their patience was wearing thin. Even the fat and good-natured Ah Lee had grown snappy. And his cooking was for once terrible.

Then at last came the moment when the young skipper, diving helmet on, went snaking down the line of the cable. He had little hope that there would be more than another rock snagged in the cable's bight.

But as he neared the bottom, he saw a shape before him that sent his heart soaring . . . the shape of a ship.

With mounting excitement he swam closer, seeking out the name on the bows. There it was at last . . . *Lexton*. They had found the wreck!

The look on his shipmates' faces when he surfaced with the news made up for a lot. But there was no time to waste on congratulations.

'We'll have to work fast,' Kaye told them. 'First we'll buoy the wreck. Then we'll have a rest. And then we'll start to work. We'll give that insurance fellow a shock.'

They were more than five miles from the original position of the wreck buoy and as they shifted it, Kaye thought it was little wonder they had failed to find the wreck. But how had the captain been so far out in his position?

A big fishing boat, a trawler, steamed by as they moored the buoy. Though it had its net down it was steaming fast and Kaye caught the glint of binoculars from its wheelhouse as it passed.

'He'll never catch anything at that speed,' Kaye remarked as he let the schooner fall away a little from the buoy before dropping anchor.

He little suspected that the trawler was later to endanger his life – and the lives of his three trusty crew mates!

They were all in need of rest and for that reason they did not moor to the buoy. Its clanging against the ship's side would have kept them awake.

Tired as he was, the young skipper had the idea in the back of his mind that there was something else odd about the trawler besides its speed but he could not place it in his mind.

It was almost dusk when the crew rose again.

'Just time for one dive,' Kaye grinned. 'I'll go down and get the hatch covers off. Then in the morning we can start work straight away.'

He had to switch on the diving helmet's light almost as soon as he passed beneath the surface. With the propeller purring he headed for the buoy and soon he was heaving himself down it towards the deck of the ship beneath.

The rusted rigging was already hung with weed. Barnacles crunched under his feet as he paced the long deserted deck. Crabs scuttled away before him as he made for the fore hatch.

Opening that hatch would normally have been the work of half-a-dozen men but with one of Kelly's gadgets, a multiple purchase block ending in a lever, the young skipper was able to hoist the sections from their places unaided.

Beneath yawned the dark cavern of the hold. Kaye took one look round him then began to clamber down.

In his mind was the thought that he would have to plan carefully to get the cargo out. The cars would be in crates, each with a lifting ring at the top. That would simplify the hoisting from above. But they would have to be hoisted in such a way that they did not crash against the hold sides. It would be useless to get them to the surface if they were damaged.

Kaye was so busy with his thoughts that he did not realise how long it was taking him to reach the cargo. The big crates should have been stacked up to fill the hold!

His feet landed on the hold deck and he looked around. He blinked and looked again.

There would be no difficulty in emptying this hold.

For there was nothing in it! Only the bare iron sides of the hold reflected back in the glow of his lamp!

Bid to Sink his Schooner!

The young skipper stood there for long moments, gazing in disbelief round the empty hold. Where had the cargo gone? How had it been removed?

Then his startled brain began to work – quickly.

He heaved himself up from the hold and made for the next hatch. Swiftly he opened it and peered in. The hold beneath was also empty.

All told a hundred cars had vanished into thin air!

Skipper Kaye's eyes were hard as he reached the steamer's deck again. There could be but the one explanation of the mystery.

The cars were not there because they had never been there! He had stumbled on a giant swindle!

'The ship and cargo were heavily insured,' he mused as he stood on the sunken deck. 'The owners have already collected the insurance money. They must have decided to make an extra profit by unloading the cars before they scuttled the ship.'

It all tied in. This explained why the *Lexton* had not been at the spot the captain had reported. He had given a wrong position for the sinking to ensure that the wreck was not found, to ensure that there would be no salvage. The *Lexton's* captain must obviously be in the cunning swindle.

'But they're not getting away with it, by thunder,' the young Skipper promised himself as he headed for the surface. 'We'll head directly for port and report to the authorities . . .'

What a sensation his story would cause, he thought. What a shock it would be for the swindlers!

Kaye was three-quarters of the way to the surface before he heard the throb of a powerful propeller close by. He craned his head back to peer upwards.

And his eyes widened in alarm.

For right above him there was outlined the shape of a ship, a ship which was heading directly for the *Dolphin*. A glance at the hull shape was enough to tell the young skipper that it was a trawler. And as he realised this a memory came back to him . . .

'That trawler I spotted. Now I know what was odd about it. It didn't have any registration numbers.'

Like motor cars, all fishing vessels have to carry registration letters and numbers so that they can be identified. But the trawler that had been fishing so fast, that steamed so close to the *Dolphin,* that had carried men who were plainly interested in the schooner – it had carried no numbers. It did not mean to be identified. That was proof that it was up to no good.

And Kaye could make a shrewd guess what it was up to.

'The captain of the *Lexton* must be aboard it,' he breathed. 'Keeping watch on the spot where he knows he sunk his ship, making sure that we don't find the wreck and uncover his racket!'

It was the only answer.

The trawler was heading directly for the *Dolphin,* obviously intending to ram and sink her. Then there would be no evidence left, no one to bear witness to the empty holds of the *Lexton*. By the time another salvage ship found the wreck it would be too late in the season to work. The insurance company would write off the cargo as a dead loss.

'And a dead loss is what we'll be,' Kaye thought grimly.

He tried to force his way upward quickly, to reach the ship before the collision took place. Yet even if he did, what could he do? He could not even clamber over the side before the collision. The *Dolphin* would sink like a stone, her side stove in.

Then, as collision seemed inevitable, Kaye saw his own ship start forward as the propeller began to turn.

'Kelly must have been running the engine,' Kaye breathed. 'And Abdullah's given him the warning.'

His heart leaped as he saw the *Dolphin* surge ahead, just far enough to dodge the onrushing stem of the trawler.

'Missed her that time,' Kaye breathed in delight.

But the trawler was turning. Faster than the schooner, it would not miss again.

Kaye saw the trawler's propeller stop and then go astern. It was turning quickly for a second attack.

When it passed right above him, Kaye saw a hope, a faint hope, of saving his ship.

The propeller on his helmet whirled at full speed. He drove his way through the water, straight towards the trawler's stern.

The massive blades of the trawler's propeller whirled and then slowed. In a moment they would stop for a second before the ship went ahead again. Could he act in time? Could he do what he planned before those whirling blades started? If he failed he would be in terrible peril. If the blades began to turn while he was still close they would suck him into their vortex, they would cut him to ribbons in an instant.

And yet it was the one hope of saving the *Dolphin*.

The young skipper did not hesitate.

He had timed his approach perfectly and as the propeller stopped turning, he pounced on it. From round his waist he pulled free a length of tough steel rope. One end he wound round the propeller shaft. The other he hooked on to the rudder. He was still hooking on when he heard the jingle of the engine room telegraph. The trawler was going ahead again.

Just in time he kicked his way clear!

The massive blades whirled into movement, their bite on the water causing a drag which almost sucked him into them.

But as the propeller turned, the steel rope tightened, winding round the shaft, pulling the ship's rudder hard over, twisting it out of shape, making the ship above swing in a tight circle.

The wire stretched taut. Could it stand the terrific strain? Then Kaye saw the propeller's beat slowing. The engine stopped.

The *Dolphin* was safe – for the moment.

At top speed Kaye headed for his ship. He reached the ladder and hoisted himself from the water. He could hear the angry voices of his crew. They were yelling at the trawler, not knowing that it had been trying deliberately to run them down.

'Call yourselves sailors!' shouted Kelly. 'Ye're not fit to push a pram.'

But their expressions changed when Kaye hauled himself aboard and told them his story.

'Why, the murdering rogues!' gasped Kelly. 'They should be behind bars.'

'And so they will,' answered the young skipper. 'Just as soon as we get ashore.'

'If you get ashore!' rasped a harsh voice from behind. 'Put up your hands the lot of you.'

A small boat had crept silently across from the trawler while Kaye was telling his story to his shipmates. Now four men lined the schooner's rail. And each of them held a gun in his hand.

Their leader had a strong, scarred face. Kaye recognised him at once as the *Lexton's* captain – Carl Bahn.

'Get below,' ordered Bahn.

'Why should we?' Kaye demanded. 'You're going to sink our ship, anyway, aren't you? We'd as soon die here on deck.'

As he spoke he edged a little closer, hands still high. The captain scowled. Plainly he was trying to nerve himself to pull the trigger. Running down a ship might be killing – but shooting in cold blood was another matter.

Yet certainly he would have fired – if he had the chance.

But before his finger could tighten on the trigger. Skipper Kaye's helmet suddenly shot forth a long, thin jet of blue-white flame. The flame had been intended for underwater cutting. It was at tremendously high pressure, hot enough to burn through inch-thick steel at a hundred fathoms. It shot near the rascally captain's knuckles – and that was enough.

With a yell Bahn dropped his gun.

Kaye flicked off the control knob on his helmet and the flame died as he sprang in with flailing fists.

The other three men were taken completely aback. For an instant their leader staggered in front of them. They could not hope to fire without hitting him.

Then Kelly and Abdullah were on them like tigers. Kelly was swinging his favourite spanner. Abdullah had no need of any other weapon than his own mighty fists.

Skipper Kaye looked on, enjoying the spectacle. Kelly launched himself at the burliest member of the trio, who was so busy avoiding the down-swinging spanner that he completely failed to notice Kelly's other fist – until it crashed with devastating force against his stubbled chin.

Mighty Abdullah let out a blood-curdling whoop – and promptly dealt with the other two men by banging their heads together!

'Let's get aboard the trawler, skipper,' begged Kelly. 'Sure I'm only just getting warmed up, and there's plenty more over there.'

'Don't be so bloodthirsty,' Kaye grinned. 'We'll leave them where they are. With their prop out of action, they won't be going any place . . . But we are. We're heading for port and a police station with these beauties.'

It was only afterwards, when the crooks had been handed over, that Kaye had time to think of the effect of the adventure.

'We've done a lot of work,' he said ruefully. 'But we haven't salvaged anything. We won't get paid a halfpenny.'

But he need not have worried. For the following day the insurance company representative came aboard – with a handsome cheque in his hand.

'You've done a great job, Skipper.' he told Kaye. 'Those crooks have confessed their guilt and have taken us to where they stored the stolen cars. So here is your reward.'

Kaye whistled as he saw the size of the cheque.

'Ah Lee,' he called. 'Let's celebrate with a feed. What can you make that's special? And we'll have a guest.'

The plump cook beamed happily as he looked at the insurance man. 'Plenty of glub,' he chuckled. 'What would you like? Flied lice?'

The insurance man went pale.

'I . . . I don't think I'll stay.'

And he never did learn that Ah Lee could not pronounce the letter 'r'.

The Stragglers

Lieutenant Commander Neville Reece was fighting mad. His ship, the destroyer Seahawk *had been sunk by a deadly U-boat attack.*

Now he stood behind a stuttering flak gun on the deck of that self-same U-boat, engaged in a hand-to-hand battle against the onslaught of a four-engined enemy aircraft.

The fate of a straggling tanker carrying 15,000 tons of fuel oil desperately needed for Britain's war effort depended on his marksmanship.

The convoy was 45 merchant ships of all shapes, tonnages and conditions, with three destroyers making up a meagre escort. These vessels steamed out of New York Harbour to take station at dawn on a grey winter's day in 1940. There was a choppy sea and heavy rain, and the sky was a sombre blue-black for as far as seamen's eyes could peer.

Aboard HMS *Seahawk,* one of the escort group, the damp gloom seemed as thick in the wardroom as it was on the rain-lashed decks.

Number One, Lieutenant Julian Aspinall, shook his head sadly. 'Greystoke's boots will take a lot to fill, Guns. Do you think this chap Reece is made of the right stuff?'

Sub-lieutenant Michael Houghton, the gunnery officer, shrugged. 'Time and the North Atlantic will tell us that . . . The Luftwaffe dealt us a cruel blow when they killed Greystoke, and I'm darned glad that my boys were able to bag the 'plane responsible.'

'Aye, but that's small consolation, Guns,' broke in Chief Engineer Ted Pendlebury. 'Greystoke was one in a million and I doubt if any of us will serve under the likes of him again. He was this vessel's nerve centre, you know . . . All good destroyer skippers are like that. They become part of their command itself.'

'I think you're right there, Chief,' nodded Aspinall thoughtfully. 'But remember – these days a man's vessel can be ripped apart by torpedoes before he has the chance to get the feel of it. It's not trials we're headed for . . .'

On the *Seahawk's* exposed bridge the new captain, Lieutenant-Commander Neville Reece, gripped the salt-stained steel coaming, narrowing his eyes as the wind and the rain beat viciously into his grey face.

The ocean that lay before him was the desolate scene of a grim battle that had been bitterly fought from the moment the declaration of war had been signed. Island Britain depended upon the maintenance of her Atlantic sea lanes for food and supplies. Therefore her fate was in the hands of the Navy and the Merchant Service . . . convoys like this one that confronted the perils of marauding U-boats, surface raiders and long-range bombers. All this, and of course, the cruel sea.

Reece wondered just how many British ships had never finished their crossings, but had slipped below the waves to watery graves at the bottom of the ocean. It was a chilling thought when the next ship could be yours . . .

Long days of ceaseless vigilance, fraught with tension and uncertainty, had passed before one of the merchant ships, the *Dowcester Victory,* a tanker carrying 15,000 tons of fuel oil, developed engine trouble.

The Convoy Commander decided it would be folly to reduce the whole convoy to half-speed, for these waters were U-boat hunting grounds and many cargoes vital to Britain's war effort might well be forfeited if they were attacked.

Therefore the *Dowcester Victory* would have to drop out of the convoy. There was no alternative. But the oil she carried was desperately needed, and it would be pitiful to leave her as helpless prey for the merciless German submarines. Reluctantly, because he could scarcely afford a reduced escort, the Commander gave orders for the *Seahawk* to stay behind with the straggling tanker.

By nightfall the *Seahawk* and the *Dowcester Victory* were alone, heaving gently over the long black rollers of the Atlantic, while above them a full moon played hide and seek behind scudding dark clouds.

Reece and Aspinall were on the destroyer's bridge talking quietly.

'How are the men reacting, Number One?' Reece asked. He had now been aboard the *Seahawk* long enough to have learnt that, basically, she was a happy ship where the crew liked and respected their officers and there was no need for feelings to be hidden.

Aspinall grinned. 'Well, they're a plucky, loyal bunch, sir, as you'll find out. But just now they're apprehensive. They think we're bound to attract trouble out on our own like this.

Reece breathed deeply. 'Yes, we're sitting ducks all right,' he said softly, and fell silent.

When trouble came, it was heralded by a tell-tale *ping* in the alert ears of the Asdic operator.

'Asdic contact to starboard bow, sir! Moving in fast!'

Then suddenly the starboard lookout gave a shout of alarm. 'Torpedoes to starboard!'

And it was the lookout's cry that jerked Reece into action. His eyes picked out the two streaks of compressed air bubbles . . . and the awful truth struck home. 'Good grief! They're already taking pot shots at us!'

He bent over the voice pipes and rapped out orders. 'Action stations! Hard a-starb'd, coxswain! Chief, give it all she's got!'

But, fast as Reece had given his orders, the *Seahawk* was taking evasive action too late! Although the destroyer was beginning to swing round, the torpedoes were now very close indeed and they were obviously not going to be dodged. Reece felt a bitter, futile fury mounting within him.

The German torpedoes slammed home astern. There was a violent explosion and a great gout of water shot skywards, milky white in the moonlight.

As the sea gushed in through the *Seahawk's* ruptured plates, men clambered up to the decks in all states of dress and alarm – and they brought with them reports of extensive damage.

On the bridge, with his ship settling beneath him, Neville Reece moved towards an agonising decision.

Aspinall advised him of the situation. 'Sir, we're taking water fast and the pumps are next to useless! They can't cope . . .'

Momentarily Reece hesitated. Then he smashed a clenched fist hard into the palm of his left hand. 'Very well, Number One. Give the order to abandon ship!'

It was the unhappiest moment of his life.

Aboard the heavily laden, lumbering *Dowcester Victory,* young First Mate

Ronald Billings saw the *Seahawk's* crew jumping for hastily lowered life-boats and Carley floats as their ship took on a heavy list to starboard.

'Great Scott!' he gasped. 'The destroyer's sinking, sir! The Navy's taking to the boats!'

But Captain Adam Bolt was pointing a thick finger to port. 'Look, Mr Billings,' he said gruffly, 'the U-boat's surfacing!'

Through his night glasses Bolt could see the water streaming off the glistening black back of the German submarine. Men scrambled up through the hatch of the conning tower.

Billings turned fearful eyes on his skipper. 'What's it to be, sir? We're a floating powder keg. One torpedo and we'll be blasted to dust!'

'Keep calm, lad! Sound the siren and get the gun manned . . .'

The *Dowcester Victory* buzzed with nervous activity. In the wheelhouse, Captain Bolt crouched low, his gnarled hand tight about the 'phone connecting him with the ship's one gunnery position on the poop deck.

'What the devil's the swab playing at?' he muttered as the throb of the U-boat's diesels came louder over the waves. 'If he gets much closer he'll be within fire range.'

Then the submarine's engines were stopped and Bolt and Billings saw the gun crew pout out eagerly on the deck, glad no doubt to breath the fresh air and feel salt spray on their pale faces. Billings' heart sank with a lurch as they filed forward to their deck gun.

'What shall we do, sir? If we head off under full steam, the Jerries will loose off a torpedo; if we stay put, we'll be bombarded with shells – '

'But at least we'll get a chance to hit back with our twelve-pounder if we stay close-in, lad! If we have to go down, we'll do it showing our teeth!'

The veteran merchant sea captain rang the engine room telegraph to full ahead, a bold light shining in his clear grey eyes. 'Helmsman, hard to port! We'll go in and meet the blighter. That should startle him!'

The *Dowcester Victory* swung round ponderously, carving a boiling, arc-shaped wake through the Atlantic rollers.

The U-boat's diesels pounded into life again as the vessel was hastily manoeuvred to dodge the charging tanker.

Bolt rapped instructions to his gun crew. 'We'll be running parallel to target any moment – prepare to fire!'

The first shells left the two vessels almost simultaneously. The Nazi gunners had better luck. Their shell struck home and the wheelhouse of the *Dowcester Victory* disintegrated in a screaming chaos of flying wood and glass.

Ron Billings and Captain Bolt were thrown off their feet by the thunderous explosion.

Bolt was mortally wounded.

While the attention of the U-boat captain and his crew was riveted on the destruction of the tanker, a lifeboat was creeping up daringly on the U-boat's blind side.

There were seven men aboard including Lieutenant-Commander Reece, Lieutenant Aspinall, Sub-lieutenant Houghton and Chief Engineer Pendlebury. Aspinall sat high in the stern facing for'ard; Reece was slumped low alongside him, quietly seething with anger.

'Come on, lads!' Aspinall urged the men who plied the oars. 'Let's give the merchant blokes a hand. The *Seahawk* may be gone, but the Navy's not finished yet! Pull, pull!'

Eventually the rowers shipped oars and let the lifeboat drift gently alongside the U-boat's stern. Aspinall chuckled softly. 'The Jerries are so busy congratulating themselves, they haven't bothered to keep tabs on us! Chief, you go for'ard with Kenner and Miles and deal with that gun crew. The rest of us will take the tower!'

Chief Engineer Ted Pendlebury cautiously led his party behind the cover of the U-boat's conning tower. They saw the jubilant Nazi gunners pointing and laughing.

'When the fire reaches the oil – '

'Ja! What an explosion there will be!'

Gleefully intent on the unhappy predicament of the *Dowcester Victory,* the Germans had no warning of the boarders until a hoarse shout rent the air.

'*At 'em, men!*'

Ted Pendlebury and his two helpers threw themselves on to the startled gun crew.

On the U-boat's bridge, the commander and his first officer turned their heads in stunned surprise.

'Zum teufel! What . . .?'

'The Englanders from the destroyer, Herr Kapitan!'

In their amazement at the unexpected scene by the deck gun, the pair did not notice that Aspinall was climbing up the steel rungs on the side of the conning tower. Filled with anger, the captain drew his revolver and levelled it at Pendlebury's back. 'Quickly, Kaufmann! Shoot the hotheads down. There are only three!' But before he could pull the trigger, Aspinall was vaulting over the rail behind him.

The *Seahawk's* Number One hit the German hard on the jaw as he turned. The first officer was dealt with in like manner by Houghton who followed Aspinall on to the bridge.

With surprise on their side, the triumphant British boarders dropped through the conning tower hatch and burst dramatically into the control room, captured guns drawn.

The confused German crew found themselves prisoners under the guard of British ratings before they could take stock of the situation. While more of the *Seahawk's* crew completed the take-over operation, Aspinall addressed Reece.

'Sir, with your permission I plan to man this sub and escort the *Dowcester Victory* until we're within range of Coastal Command aircraft from home.'

A gleam of satisfaction made Reece's eyes sparkle 'Well done, Number One. It sounds a good idea. Go ahead!'

After a fashion, the assault on the U-boat and its capture were a compensation for the loss of their destroyer. Reece could tell that this was the way the *Seahawk's* survivors saw it. But Reece was the descendant of a long line of professional sailors, and a man steeped in naval tradition – and pride. The German's destruction of the *Seahawk* had left him with a deep-seated anger that demanded a more violent revenge than this . . .

This was only the beginning, and there were many hundreds of miles of bleak ocean before they were home.

Due to the prompt firefighting efforts of her crew and despite the sad loss of her gallant captain, the *Dowcester Victory* had survived the encounter with the U-boat, and for two days she limped across the ocean with her faulty engine and strange escort. Both vessels maintained a strict radio silence, lest a request for assistance should be overheard by enemy ears.

After those two days had passed they were within range of Coastal Command in Northern Ireland and Julian Aspinall gave instructions for an SOS call to be transmitted, giving their position and asking for immediate air cover.

But even then the stragglers were not safe, for fate took a wicked hand in their fortunes. The call was picked up by a prowling Focke-Wulf Condor of the German Luftwaffe.

The pilot was outraged. A captured U-boat! Ach, they would teach these insolent Britishers a bitter lesson! The long-range enemy aircraft changed course and soon was sighting the two vessels.

Seamen on the decks of the tanker heard the roar of the Condor's four powerful engines and turned their eyes skywards apprehensively.

'Heck! It's a Jerry – now we're really for it!'

With bomb doors open the 'plane howled in on the tanker and the seamen saw a stick of three bombs falling. In the ship's damaged wheelhouse Ron Billings shouted orders urgently. 'Hard-a-port, helmsman. Now!'

The three bombs sent up huge cascades of water as they plunged into the sea, close to the ship. Then the Condor was zooming away, its path carrying it over the U-boat . . . where a gunner from the *Seahawk* was ready behind the submarine's flak gun!

Hot lead ripped into the aircraft and the angry pilot realised that before he could deal with the virtually unarmed tanker, he would have to take care of the U-boat's gun. The Condor came round again, low, with machine guns hammering, and the man from the *Seahawk* was thrown back from the gun in a hail of bullets.

The German pilot grunted his satisfaction, but as the aircraft climbed away, the co-pilot saw a second man, dragging the dead man aside and taking up position behind the gun.

'Herr Lieutenant, there is a second gunner. Himmel! These foolhardy Britishers . . .!'

When Neville Reece saw the gunner tumble in a grotesque huddle to the U-boat's deck, he darted forward to take his place unhesitatingly and without thought or fear.

Three days earlier he might not have done so, but now he was an avenging fury. Since the sinking of the *Seahawk,* his whole system had demanded violent action against the hated enemies who had deprived him of his command. And here was his chance!

Reece saw the big German 'plane come round and once more whine down determindly on the U-boat, guns chattering. Now it was his turn, even as it had been the gunner's. He felt the bullets tear into his flesh, but he clenched his teeth and fought off the blackness that threatened to suck up his senses like an evil bog.

But the Condor seemed flak-proof. It clawed its throbbing way across the sky and turned yet again. Then it was making its fourth approach.

Reece saw the big German 'plane come round and once more whine down determinedly on the U-boat, guns chattering.

It loomed into Reece's hazy vision with a clarity that astonished him. Automatically he followed it round again with the stuttering flak gun.

'Must get him this time . . . mustn't pass out.'

Reece did not witness the violent explosion amidships the Condor. Nor did he see the flames that transformed the doomed machine into a hurtling fireball as they found fuel. He did not see his target plunge into the ocean, streaming flame.

He must, however, have come round quite quickly after that. For he remembered seeing the spreading white wings of frothing water on the sea's surface, the countless bubbles and patch of floating oil that marked the aircraft's end.

Aspinall was leaning over him, his face filled with grave concern.

'Sir! Are you all right, sir?'

Reece smiled. 'I got the blighter, Number One!' he said exultantly. Then he added curiously, 'It did me good.'

As far as Aspinall could see, the Condor's machine guns had done Reece a great deal of harm, but he did not have the chance to hear his skipper explain his strange words. After he had spoken, Reece slumped back again, unconscious.

With the destroyer captain's great act of valour behind the flak gun, the convoy straggler's ordeal had reached its climax. Not long after, a Catalina flying-boat from Northern Ireland arrived to carry Reece off to land and hospital. It was the final curtain. Admiring officers and men lined the decks of the U-boat and the tanker to watch him go.

'Well, that's that,' murmured Chief Engineer Ted Pendlebury. 'Pity we lost the *Seahawk*, though. Reece would have made a mighty fine skipper in time. Had the right spirit, y'know . . .'

The Fabulous Spider

Colonel Phinn, head of World Security, started to speak tersely.

'Pablo Kruzo, the notorious dictator, has absconded with the best part of his country's wealth and treasures. We want him brought here alive – but he has built himself an impregnable fortress with all scientific aids to security. Only you, spider, can carry out this impossible mission.'

He waited for a reply. The amazing Spider sneered and shook his sleek head.

'No,' he replied.

Against the night sky of New York's Manhattan district towered the slim skyscraper that housed United World Security, a secret-service agency serving many Western nations. Its glittering walls were lit by the glow of the great city, but nobody noticed the strange figure which swarmed swiftly up the sheer walls, passing lighted office windows.

The Spider, formerly notorious as a criminal genius, now using his talents as the world's most fantastic crime-fighter, was climbing to the top floor.

Using his amazing artificial web-apparatus, he spun his way upwards like a giant insect, a sneering smile on his lean, angular face.

'They ask for my help,' he muttered, 'but even now there are those who would like to trap the Spider. Fools!'

In his quiet, air-conditioned office on the top floor, Colonel Amos Phinn, head of World Security, tapped his desk impatiently. For the twentieth time he spoke into his office inter-com.

'No sign of the Spider yet?'

'No sir,' his secretary replied. 'A messenger is standing by in the vestibule to bring him to you immediately he arrives.'

'Humph!' Phinn glanced at his watch. 'Not like the Spider to be late! I hope he hasn't let me down!'

The hair on the back of his neck stirred. He felt a chill breeze, coming straight off the Hudson River, and into the quiet of the office came the muted roar of New York's traffic.

He swung his chair round and gasped in amazement. The Spider was standing in the room, and the square of glass removed from the window with furtive silence showed how he had entered.

'Good evening, Colonel Phinn,' said the bizarre, black-clad figure with a sardonic grin.

'Why? *Why*?' Phinn groaned. 'Why choose this extraordinary method of entering my office?'

The Spider smiled. 'Just to make sure there was no trap, Colonel! I am suspicious of everybody!'

'You've no need to fear me,' Phinn rasped. 'I want your help!' He flicked the inter-com switch down again, and said with a sigh: 'Relax, Miss Fortman. The Spider is here!'

He smiled slightly as the inter-com crackled. 'Yes, yes, I know you didn't see or hear him – but the Spider is an amazing man!'

'My time is valuable,' snapped the Spider, using a small laser gun to fuse the glass back into the window. 'State your problem, Colonel!'

Aware of the amazing talents of the man he had called to his office, Colonel Phinn started to speak tersely. Pablo Kruzo, dictator of a small country in Central America, had absconded with the best part of his country's wealth and its treasures, which had been bought by him over the years with money paid as taxes by his people. World Security had discovered that he had fled to a small island republic in the Caribbean.

The Spider shrugged. 'Get him out, then!'

'Impossible! We have no extradition treaty with these people, and Kruzo has the corrupt government under his thumb!'

'Well, send your clever agents to spirit him away,' the Spider sneered. 'This seems to be no task for a man of my genuis! I must go. I have other, more important things to do!'

'Wait! It's impossible for ordinary men to reach him,' the Colonel pleaded. 'Kruzo has built himself an impregnable fortress with all scientific aids to security!'

'This business is no concern of mine,' the Spider said loftily, moving to the door. 'The miserable peasants of his country mean nothing to me. Your organisation must look after them!'

Desperately the Colonel played his trump card. 'But Kruzo plans to set himself up as the greatest criminal brain in the world. Using his resources, he can defeat every criminal boss –.'

The Spider turned, his strange eyes glittering.

'Impertinence!' he snarled. 'I am still the greatest criminal genius the world has ever seen, even if I have now turned my fantastic talent to the aid of the forces of law and order.'

Colonel Phinn knew he had touched the Spider's enormous vanity.

'You will co-operate, then?' he asked eagerly.

'I leave at once,' the Spider snapped, and spoke tersely into the microphone of his radio telephone. 'Professor Pelham, you may land the helicar on the roof of the World Security building.'

Professor Pelham and Roy Ordini, the Spider's assistant, had been waiting, hovering over the skyscraper in the Spider's silent, speedy, aerial vehicle.

'We have a mission in the Caribbean,' the Spider snapped as he stepped into the helicar. 'We will use the hydrofoil. I do not propose to waste much time on Pablo Kruzo!'

Pablo Kruzo, plump, olive-skinned, dressed in a colourful military uniform, with medals and orders clanking on his chest, chuckled as he sat at his desk in his island fortress.

'Now I await the Spider,' he boasted. 'He is the only man in the world worthy to challenge my ambitions! The defences are all ready?'

'The Spider cannot approach this island without being sighted by Government forces, Excellency,' his aide said smoothly. 'And even if he gets past them, we are ready here!'

'Good!' Kruzo rubbed his fat hands together. 'Once the Spider is disposed of, there will be no threat to my plans to dominate world crime!'

At that moment the Spider's hydrofoil boat hummed towards the island at an incredible speed. Its hull was lifted right out of the water, and its wake creamed behind it for miles.

Roy Ordini was at the wheel. The Spider sat on a deckhouse stool, arms folded, a thin smile on his lips. Professor Pelham, his hair wild, sat at a complex bank of instruments.

'Where shall we land, boss?' asked Ordini.

'At the main quay in the harbour, of course,' the Spider snapped. 'You have picked up their signals, Professor?'

'Their radar has been tracking us in for some time, Spider,' the Professor smiled. 'Do you wish me to jam it?'

'Naturally not! Unless, of course, they open fire at us,' the Spider shrugged. 'But I do not think they will do that! You have traced Kruzo's lair, Professor?'

'Yes, I have taken a bearing, picked up from the electronic machines he has installed,' Pelham chuckled. 'It is that old castle on the hilltop above the port!'

The Spider's glittering eyes stared ahead. 'Yes, I see it! A simple matter to approach it, gentlemen!'

'Could be you're underestimating this Kruzo guy, boss . . .' said Ordini, hesitantly.

'Rubbish! I've no doubt Kruzo is a capable enough villain,' the Spider scowled, 'but he has no hope of defeating me! Kruzo's Island . . . how pitiful that he should think he can escape me by hiding here!'

The hydrofoil surged into the harbour and dropped gradually on to its hull as Ordini cut the power. It swept up to the quay, and the engines died as Ordini and Pelham tied up swiftly.

The Spider stepped ashore. The quay seemed empty, but as he strolled forward nonchalantly, armed troops sprang from the cover of warehouses and dockside equipment.

'Have the hose ready, Roy,' the Spider said calmly.

A tough-looking officer, gun in hand, strode towards the Spider as his troops closed in. He could not disguise the triumph in his expression.

'You are under arrest, for entering our country without permission, Señor Spider,' he barked. 'You will come with me to military headquarters!'

'Indeed?' sneered the Spider. 'You are over-optimistic, my friend!'

In a swift movement he pulled down a small face-mask over his nostrils and mouth. At that instant, Roy, who had been fiddling with the nozzle control of a thick hose, as if about to wash down the deck, swung it high.

Nobody had noticed him. All eyes had been on the sinister, black-clad figure of the amazing Spider. Not water, but a thin vapour, gushed out under high pressure, enveloping the Spider and the soldiers.

Not a man was missed by the high-pressure spray. They gasped, reeled, eyes rolling, and toppled on to the stones of the quay. Inert, they lay sprawled, eyes staring at the sky.

The Spider stood among them, smiling. 'Poor fools! Did they think to catch the Spider so easily? Well, they will be stunned for six hours, and by that time we shall be gone!'

Frightened people watched from cover as he switched on his web-machine and soared on the tough strands to the roof of a warehouse. From here, the Spider worked his way across the town, sending panic through the islanders wherever he appeared.

Behind him, Roy Ordini and Professor Pelham shot out of the hold of the hydrofoil in the helicar, swooping high over the town and making for Kruzo's stronghold. Their orders were to await the Spider's signal.

The fantastic crime-fighter was spinning his way across the tree-tops of the jungle surrounding Kruzo's fortress. A machine-gun crew awaiting in a clearing by the road to the castle saw him too late.

The Spider swooped, and a small hand-gun spat. Tiny darts tipped with a nerve-numbing preparation sprayed the startled gunners. They stiffened, paralysed by the drug which was the Spider's own invention. They would remain in this condition for an hour.

The Spider dealt stealthily with other similar outposts. He came to an electrified fence, and sneered as his laser gun cut it into sparking, flashing remnants leaving gaps wide enough to drive a truck through.

'This fellow Kruzo must do better than this!' he murmured. 'No doubt these are only his outer defences! The choice titbits are still to come!'

He saw the helicar hovering high over the castle, and heard the Professor's reply to his signal.

'Nobody in sight, Spider. No more gun posts visible from here. Take care!'

'I propose to enter the stronghold,' the Spider snapped. 'We shall see whether Kruzo can win the battle of wits and technology. What am I saying? Of course he cannot win!'

Pablo Kruzo sat alone in the very centre of his stronghold. He sat on a tiny tiled island, in the middle of a huge, domed chamber, surrounded by a deep moat which was slowly filling with a liquid which gave off faint fumes and vapour.

He chuckled as he stared at a screen in the electronic console before him.

'You have walked into my trap, Spider,' he said gloatingly. 'The defences you conquered so easily were there only to lull you into a false sense of security! All I have to do now is to wait!'

The Spider walked unchallenged through corridors and passages in the

A metallic voice boomed into the chamber. 'How do you like my little pets, Spider? They are hungry, I assure you.'

ancient castle. He knew by the silence and the complete lack of signs of human life that a trap was being prepared for him.

But the amazing man who had been the world's greatest criminal genius felt no fear. His extraordinary talents and overwhelming vanity assured him that no opponent could resist for long.

He stepped into a circular stone chamber, eyes questing. Suddenly he heard the faint humming of machinery, and the walls were covered by a steel shell which slid into place. The door was hidden, and he was standing in a steel cylinder the diameter of a small room.

'Kruzo is watching me,' he thought. 'Now what?'

His answer came as his feet dropped away into emptiness. The floor had vanished. He fell into darkness, unable to use his web projector, until he landed on something that twanged in the darkness like rubber. Thick strands held him. He did not bounce off the rubbery substance, but sprawled there helplessly, gripped by something like powerful glue.

For a moment the Spider lay there. There was enough light for him to see that he had fallen into a vast spider's web. But it was like no other web he had ever seen, for the strands were as thick as a man's arm, and despite all his efforts, he could not tear himself away from their sticky grip.

The Spider glanced round, hearing a loud, creaking and rustling. It was a moment of sheer horror, even for the iron-nerved crimefighter.

Advancing on him were four giant spiders. Their bodies were at least six feet long, and their giant legs creaked and grated as they scuttled swiftly towards him.

'Great webs of death!' he muttered. 'This Kruzo is a foe after my own heart! He has chosen to fight me, the Spider, with spiders of his own. And what huge, loathsome creatures they are!'

A metallic voice boomed into the chamber. 'How do you like my little pets, Spider? They are hungry, I assure you. You have but seconds to live . . . time to think of your folly!'

'Pah! You are a fool, Kruzo. A good idea, I'll admit. But not good enough to beat the Spider!'

The Spider was gripped immovably by the monster spider's web. All except his right hand – and this hand held his laser gun. He turned the searing beam on the web around him, and it sizzled away with a pungent smell. He dropped, but still one hand was held fast, and he swung, legs kicking.

The spiders were making twittering noises as they creaked towards the centre of the web. Still the Spider was in danger.

But again and again he fired his laser gun. He watched as the searing beam hit the spiders one by one. They burst into flame, shrivelled like burning brown paper, and fell through the gaps in the web.

Burning fragments lay below him as he used the gun to free himself from the final grip of the death web. Then he dropped lightly to the floor of the chamber.

'I have dealt with the villain's last trap,' he barked over his mini-radio. 'Pelham and Ordini, be prepared to enter the roof and take Kruzo away. He cannot escape me now!'

The Spider saw an open doorway leading into a tunnel. He strode along this, and came out on to a circular parapet in a huge, domed chamber. A broad moat, with vapour wisping from it, separated him from Pablo Kruzo, who stood on his tiny tiled island, jeering.

'I admit I didn't think you'd get past my little pets,' Kruzo snarled. 'But I warn you, Spider, the moat is filled with acid. If you try to cross it, and fall in, you will die horribly!'

'So I gather,' the Spider said calmly, watching his adversary. 'But I have come to take you away, Kruzo, and this I shall do!'

Kruzo's foot stabbed a button. The door behind the Spider closed with a hum, barring his retreat. Another button was touched, and a machine-gun on a tripod shot out of the floor of Kruzo's island. He seized the hand-grips, swinging the gun to aim at the Spider.

'One burst and you will fall into the acid,' he yelled. 'Heh, heh, the end of the mighty Spider . . . and I shall be King of Crime!'

But the Spider had moved even faster. His web projector hissed, and strands shot across the sea of liquid. Before Kruzo could fire his gun, they whipped around him, and held him like iron bands as he struggled helplessly against their grip.

In his struggles, he tottered and reeled, and staggered back in horror as he found himself almost falling into the moat of acid.

He stood still, panting, eyes glaring, as the Spider calmly swarmed across his manufactured web, his weight sending it sagging almost to the surface of the deadly liquid.

'Stand still, Kruzo,' he said mockingly, 'and use all your strength – because if you totter forward, we shall both fall into your acid bath!'

And so Pablo Kruzo had to stand helplessly, ashen with fear, as his enemy used him as a support to climb across the deadly moat.

Suddenly, there was a loud crashing sound. Kruzo jumped in fright, and the Spider's web-bridge bounced and jogged, almost shaking the famous crime-buster from his precarious perch. But he hung on like a limpet.

'You cowardly fool!' snapped the Spider. 'I told you to stand still! That sound was merely my friends Ordini and Pelham, making their way into your stronghold via the roof-tops!' Kruzo froze once again . . . .

He was still unable to move as the Spider reached the island and both watched a section of the domed roof fall away, burned by the intruments in the helicar, and drop sizzling into the acid.

The helicar swooped down through the aperture, and came to rest on the island.

'Take him away,' said the Spider contemptuously, as Pablo Kruzo, still entwined in the coils of the steely-strong web, collapsed in a dead faint.

'What about his loot, chief?' asked Roy Ordini.

The spider shrugged.

"We'll deliver it to this fellow's unhappy country,' he said calmly. 'The poor serfs he has swindled may get some benefit from it. We do not need it!'

And bearing the man he had come to find, the Spider's helicar soared high over Kruzo's island and sped towards the waiting hydrofoil.

Go-Go Gubbins

Hereward Lancelot Gubbins, also known as All-Systems-Go-Gubbins, soon to be shortened to Go-Go Gubbins, had one consuming interest – space flights and everything to do with rockets, satellites and such-like.

That's why he built his own rocket, designed – as he proudly claimed – to reach a height of not less than eight miles.

Well, the rocket took off all right – with very unexpected results!

To begin with we used to call him All-Systems-Go-Gubbins because he was so mad-keen on anything to do with space travel, rockets and sputniks and such. But it soon became shortened to Go-Go. Well, I mean, apart from his one abiding interest in anything to do with space, what could you call a chap whose mother had him named Hereward Lancelot Rob-Roy, on account of *her* abiding interest in life was reading romantic historical novels?

Anyway, Go-Go Gubbins was his name, and the only books he ever read were science-fiction novels, and the reports of various space flights, flying saucers and satellites in orbit. There is no doubt that Go-Go had the makings of a real scientific egg-head. His mother had hoped that he would turn into another Sir Walter Scott or a Charles Kingsley, and become famous as an author of historical novels, but the idea of having to read one to find out what it was all about, only brought Go-Go out in a heat-rash.

Old Mr Ranshaw, a retired watchmaker, who lived in the largest house in our neighbourhood, let Go-Go use a large shed he had in the grounds of the house as his work-shop. It was here that Go-Go built some really good models of rockets, sputniks and jet planes which actually flew and which Go-Go controlled by means of short-wave radio.

Go-Go was not the sort to make any close friends, but I supoose I was the one who came nearest to being his best friend. I liked him in a sort of patronising way, although science-fiction was not my cup of tea, and the idea of zooming round in space, laid out in a sort of super-mobile coffin, always gave me a touch of the dreaded nadgers. To fly a jet was my ambition, and until they invented one that could be *flown* to the moon, space could wait.

Then one day Go-Go told me that he had just started on his latest rocket and greatest work; he was building a rocket which he hoped would reach a height of nine or ten miles, and he was actually working on the idea of including a radio so that he could bring the spent canister – 'vehicle' he called it – back to where he had launched it.

Soon after he had started work on the project, as Go-Go termed it, I went with him to have a look. We were met outside the shed by Mr Ranshaw himself, who had always taken a keen interest in what Go-Go was doing.

'I'm afraid,' said Mr Ranshaw, 'that I shan't be able to see the completion of your biggest work, young Gubbins.'

'Oh, indeed, sir,' said Go-Go. 'I'm sorry to hear that.'

'No. You see my married daughter has at last persuaded me that I'm a foolish old man to keep this house going, living in it all by myself. It's much too big for me, she says. Well – I shall be leaving soon to go and live with her, and I've let the house to a Mr Vesey.'

Go-Go's jaw dropped. 'Oh,' he said, looking at the shed which held all his dreams, like someone giving a last look at his own arm or leg which is about to be amputated.

'But I shouldn't worry,' said Mr Ranshaw, reading Go-Go's mind. 'I expect my tenant will be willing to let you continue using the shed. At least until you have finished on your latest project.'

Go-Go was genuinely sorry that Mr Ranshaw was leaving the district, but he was even more worried as to whether the new tenant would allow him to go on using the shed or not. During the four or five days between Mr Ranshaw's departure and the arrival of Mr Vesey, Go-Go's conversation with me consisted entirely of his giving me reasons why this Mr Vesey should allow him, Go-Go, to go on using the shed. You would have thought the fate of the nation depended on it, the reasons Go-Go thought up.

The day the new tenant arrived Go-Go asked me to go round with him to give him moral support when he made his request. Close to Mr Ranshaw's house, one of those new factories had been built, a small one, but completely modern with lots of neatly kept lawns with flower beds around the place and surrounded by a tall wire-mesh fence. Part of the grounds were separated from Mr Ranshaw's big garden by only a brick wall with barbed wire on top. There were a number of small outbuildings apart from the main building, and Go-Go looked at these wistfully.

'I wonder,' he said, 'if the worst came to the worst, whether the factory people would let me use one of their sheds?'

I thought it most unlikely but to stop him listing all the reasons why they should, I said: 'Of course they would.'

Still with that wistful look on his face, such as a little kid gives another little kid who has an ice-lolly and who won't give him a a lick, Go-Go continued to eye the small factory and its grounds as we went through the gate and up to the house.

As things turned out, the worst was even worse than Go-Go expected. As we went through the grounds towards the house we had to pass the shed, and what should we see as we approached it, but Go-Go's tools and equipment lying in an untidy heap outside the door.

Go-Go stopped dead in his tracks, his face turning a ghastly white. As we stood there, a long cylindrical object, made of light metal, suddenly sailed out through the doorway and landed longways across some iron railings. It fell back to the path bent and dented, and bursting at its welded seams.

Go-Go gave a shriek and rushed towards the wounded cylinder with arms outstretched like a demented miser who sees his gold suddenly sprout legs and run off.

Some more bits of metal of all shapes and sizes followed the cylinder out of the doorway, sailing through the air and falling about the crouching Go-Go like big leaves blown from a tree by a gale.

Go-Go ignored them all, even when one piece landed flatly on his head, giving forth a dull metallic sound. I am still to be convinced that the sound came from the metal and not from Go-Go's head.

However, the shower of metal coming out of the door ceased as suddenly as it began, and was followed by a man who wore an irritable look.

He was a youngish man with a rather large nose, a thin-lipped mouth and small eyes. When he saw Go-Go sitting on the ground and nursing the battered cylinder like a mother crooning over her babe, his lips clamped into an even thinner line.

He took two or three quick, angry paces towards Go-Go, and at the same time I took two or three quick, but not angry paces backwards, to take me out

Mr Vesey's eyes narrowed in anger. He bent towards Go-Go and said 'Get off my property at once. And take your rubbish with you.'

of range, as it were.

'I suppose you are this . . . this boy Gubbins, Mr Ranshaw told me about?' the man said. He said the word 'boy' as if he were spitting out a nasty taste in his mouth.

Go-Go looked up at the man, his round pink face stricken. 'Yuh-yes, sir,' he said.

'Well, you can get this rubbish out of my shed – right now! Mr Ranshaw told me about you, and hoped I'd let you go on using the place. I told him I couldn't consider it, and that I expected the shed to be cleared of all your rubbish by the time I arrived. As it wasn't, I've seen to it myself. And if you want any of it, you'd better get it out of my way now – this instant – or I'll put it in the dust-bins for the dustmen.'

'Bub-but if you wuh-would only allow me to fir-finish. . . .'

Mr Vesey's eyes, small as they were, grew even smaller as they narrowed in anger. He bent towards Go-Go and said from between clenched teeth, 'Get off my property at once. And take your rubbish with you.'

He straightened up, and turned and walked towards the house. At the door he turned. 'I'll give you five minutes to get out,' he shouted.

Another man and a woman appeared in the open doorway. The three of them spoke together in low tones; the other man and the woman gave us a look, which to me was very off-putting, and then all of them entered the house.

The door slammed. Poor Go-Go moaned. Here was his latest and greatest project, lying in ruins about his feet. Well, I mean, it would have been, if he hadn't been *sitting among* all the bits and pieces.

'Come on, Go-Go,' I said at last. 'We'd better get out of here. I'll help you carry this load of old cods-wallop – I mean – if you think it's worth while.' This remark brought Go-Go to his feet. He looked at me fiercely. 'Of course it's worth while,' he said.

'Well, come on then. I don't know where you're going to put it all. I remember you told me your mother won't have any of it near your house, because you don't look like turning into a writer of historical novels.'

Go-Go looked stricken again. Then his face brightened, and he took me by the arm in a friendly sort of way. I knew what was coming. 'No,' I said. 'Not under any circumstances will I have this . . . all this stuff at my place.'

I thought ruefully of my determined words an hour later, when we had just finished stowing the stuff in my Dad's shed at the bottom of our garden. It was the end of a harrowing sixty minutes, for it was unfortunate for us, and particularly for Go-Go, that a number of the boys of our neighbourhood had heard and seen the business between Mr Vesey and Go-Go. And they were all in the street waiting to cheer us on as we came out of the gate of Mr Ranshaw's house, loaded like beasts of burden, with all manner of weird contraptions. Although Go-Go did not look so much like a beast of burden as a walking metal chimney stack which had received the worst of the argument with a bad-tempered gale.

The boys went with us all the way to my house, cheering and laughing, and suggesting that someone should light a fire under Go-Go in order that smoke might issue forth from the chimney. Poor old Go-Go was the laughing stock of the neighbourhood.

'Go-Go's gone and been sent-sent-sent!' they chanted. 'And he's been and got his chimney bent-bent-bent!'

We stayed in my Dad's shed until the boys outside the garden got tired of waiting for us to come out. When the last of them had drifted homewards and just before he left, Go-Go said: 'You won't have to hang on to this lot for long – I mean – my apparatus. I'll have it moved in a day or two!'

'You'd better,' I answered gloomily. 'Or my Dad will move it – and me – with his boot.'

I did not find out at the time what persuasion Go-Go used to get his mother to let him take it to their small garden, but that's what happened the very next day. The day after, Go-Go told me he was in production again – using his mother's greenhouse.

For two or three weeks we hardly saw Go-Go after school – he was busy, doggedly repairing the damage done by Mr Vesey, and progessing in the construction of his rocket.

Then, one Friday, Go-Go announced that the rocket was ready for launching and that, indeed, the count-down would take place the next morning on the Common behind the new factory.

'You can all,' said Go-Go as if conferring a favour, 'come and see the count-down and ascent from the launching-pad.'

Well, of course, everyone took it as a big joke. We all knew Go-Go *was* brainy and that one day he might even be a famous scientist. But he did go a bit far at times, and just asked for his leg to be pulled. Anyway, he pressed two or three of us to help him get the rocket to the launching site, and when, full of giggles, we arrived at his house the following morning, our giggles were suddenly silenced by what we saw.

He had built a most beautiful looking rocket, about six feet long, and shaped exactly as the rockets people have been sending up to miss the moon. Painted along its whole length was the inscription 'Charles Kingsley the

First'. He had named his rocket after a famous historical novelist and that explained why his mother had allowed him to use her greenhouse. I was lost in admiration of the low cunning unexpectedly displayed by Go-Go in thinking up this solution to his problem.

He had also built a sort of scaffolding – to give vertical support to the rocket before blast-off – fixed to a sheet of asbestos, and this, he informed us, was the actual launching pad. The whole assembly looked jolly convincing. He had even built a transporter – an orange box with four old pram wheels fixed to it – to get the rocket and launching pad to the scene of the operation.

When we got to the Common I was surprised to see that most of the school had turned up to watch and to have a good laugh, and there were even a reporter and a photographer.

We watched with open mouths as Go-Go was interviewed and had his picture taken standing by the rocket, which he had fixed into position against the scaffolding on the asbestos sheet. Like that, I must say the rocket looked most impressive, standing more than six feet high.

We were all silent as Go-Go went through the count-down procedure, checking that all his systems were go. Finally he straightened up and beamed.

'Blast-off will take place in seventeen seconds from now,' he announced. 'I have calculated that there is enough power in the rocket to take it up to a height exceeding eight miles.' We held our breath. Go-Go went to a small lever at the side of the rocket and put his thumb on it. 'The ignition mechanism,' he announced smugly. 'I constructed it on the same principle as that used in cigarette lighters.' He took a deep breath and shouted, 'Stand by!'

Then he began the final count-down. 'Ten-nine-eight-seven-six-five-four-three-two-one-ZERO!'

You could hear a pin drop. Then Go-Go's thumb pressed down on the lever. We were all waiting for the thing not to work. But it did! There was a short, sharp scraping sound, like a match being scraped on a matchbox, and this was immediately followed by a hissing sound. Go-Go, trying not to appear too hurried, stepped away from the rocket rather quickly.

The hissing grew louder, and suddenly smoke and flame appeared from the bottom of the rocket, in a powerful jet. A second later – and the rocket was moving upwards. It started off fairly slowly, but gathered speed rapidly.

Once we had got over our surprise, we gave a cheer.

The rocket was about one hundred feet up. 'It will soon be just a small speck in the sky,' said Go-Go excitedly, as he began fiddling with his radio-control box by which he planned to guide the falling canister back to its point of origin.

Well, well, I thought, Old Go-Go has made all these one-time jeering apes laugh on the other side of their faces . . . .

And then suddenly there was a gasp from the crowd. For the rocket, now about two hundred feet up – not as high as a good rocket soars on Guy Fawkes' night – abruptly heeled over as if an unseen hand had clouted it smartly behind the ear.

Suddenly it was zooming along horizontally; and then, equally suddenly, as if someone had knocked downwards sharply on its nose, it dipped towards earth.

We were all rooted where we stood as we watched the rocket plunging earthwards. Go-Go twiddled so frantically with the knobs on his radio-thing that one of them came off in his hand.

Horrified we saw the rocket smash through the skylight of the main building of the small factory, disappearing into its depths.

Poor Go-Go's face was a picture. 'Something went wrong,' he said. I have heard him make less obvious remarks. Then, his expression of misery giving way to one of sheer fright, as visions of immense sums for damage being claimed from his mother and his own arrest by the police, came to him, he set off at a blind run for the factory. I followed him because I was afraid he might be going to do himself an injury in his despair.

Having soon recovered from their sudden shock, the crowd began howling with laughter at Go-Go's expense, and with the reporter and photographer, began running after us to see the rest of the tragedy.

The man on the gate at the factory – where they did not work on a Saturday – was still staring up at the shattered skylight when we arrived, and I am certain that he was sure that a Thing from Outer Space had most unexpectedly arrived on his doorstep.

He made no effort to stop us as we dashed into the factory compound, and we were beaten by inches to the door of the building by a police car which had swept in after us.

Three hefty policemen managed to barge the door open, and the Sergeant shouted at us: 'You boys get out of here! It might go off!'

Go-Go looked as if he wished *he* could go off – as far away as possible and never be seen or heard of again. But he paid no attention to the Sergeant and followed him at a run into the building. Perhaps he had the idea of snatching up what was left of his beloved rocket from under their noses, and running off with it to the peace of a far-off sanctuary.

It was a one-storied building, divided into various workshops by wooden partitions, and the skylight was over the centre of the building. We followed the police through open doors until we came to the central section, where we saw the policemen standing just inside the doorway as if they had been frozen into statues.

From inside the room came a plaintive wail. 'It's a fair cop. We'll come quietly. Only get us out of here!'

Wide-eyed with wonder, we stooped down to get the only view we could of the interior of the room – between the policemen's legs. And there, through a thick cloud of smoke, we saw the rocket. It had embedded its nose in the wooden floor, but the force with which it had landed had burst its seams again, and it had opened out like a steel partition, cutting off one corner of the room, leaving only a small space between its right-hand edge and the wall.

Three frightened faces, one on top of the other, their eyes streaming with tears from the smoke, and coughing and spluttering every time they drew breath, peered through the narrow, smoke-filled gap. But what made *our* eyes open wider and our jaws drop lower, was the fact that these three faces belonged to Mr Vesey, his wife and her brother – as we later learned. And they had no business being in the factory, not being employed there.

When the police, helped by Go-Go and me, had removed the remains of the rocket, we found there was an open safe in the corner, and in front of it a number of papers lying on the floor.

Suddenly Mr Vesey picked up a long, thin cylindrical piece that had fallen from the inside of the burst rocket, and took a swipe at the Sergeant.

Go-Go gave an anguished cry, 'My radio control!' and launched himself at the man. Go-Go's head collided with Mr Vesey's stomach very forcibly, and it was then Mr Vesey's turn to give an anguished cry, which he did, sitting down suddenly at the same time, clutching his midriff, and moaning even more loudly than Go-Go was, as he looked at the dented cylinder he held mournfully in his hands.

Well, Mr Vesey's attack on the Sergeant – who had some difficulty in getting his helmet back up over his ears where Go-Go's cylinder in the hand of Mr Vesey had hammered it – was enough for the police to arrest all three of them.

And this was rather a good thing as it turned out, for in their pockets, when they were searched at the police station, was found the complete formula for the latest rocket fuel developed by scientists in this country. Developed, in fact, in this very factory on which Go-Go's rocket had landed. We were amazed to think that the 'factory' had been just a cover for a very hush-hush laboratory.

It appeared that Mr Vesey and his relations – had blundered into the secret of the factory. If they could only get the formula out, they could sell it to one of the many foreign countries who would be willing to pay vast sums for it.

They rented Mr Ranshaw's house; it was perfect for them to, as they say, 'case the joint', and even more easy for them to slip over the wall while the gate-keeper-cum-watchman's back was turned, and break into the main building.

Well, Go-Go had to give evidence when they were tried, and this time his picture was in the national newspapers, because if it had not been for Go-Go's rocket, the thieves would have got away with the formula, and that would have been a bad thing for us all.

By the time the papers had finished with the story of Go-Go's rocket, they made it seem that he had secret information, that thieves and traitors had broken into the place, and that by clever manipulation of his radio-control, he had aimed the rocket deliberately at the skylight, to catch them in the act.

And it didn't matter that Go-Go said it was a lot of rubbish – people would not believe him, but preferred to believe the fairy-tale in the newspapers. Well, I thought, it made up in some way for the way everyone had laughed at him in the past, for there was no doubt about it now, Go-Go was the hero of the neighbourhood. His mother even gave up the idea of his becoming an historical novelist. And this made Go-Go happier than anything else.

Who Disturbs me – Dies!

The old coin, brought up from the sea-bed had a curse on it. There it was, in Inca symbols, on the ancient doubloon. 'Who disturbs me – dies!'

The crew of the Lucky Star *were not to be deterred from their quest for undersea treasure by such a warning from the long-dead past. But then some very strange happenings began to take place. The curse was working its evil!*

Tom Stacey bobbed to the surface, snatched off his frogman's face-mask and yelled: 'Gold, fellas! I've hit it!'

Crew members of the *Lucky Star* leapt to their feet, all eyes on the figure frantically flailing at the surface of the blue Caribbean. In his hand held high aloft they could see a great yellow disc almost as big as a cocoa tin lid. In his other hand he held an ornament.

Next moment Tom was splashing towards them, too excited to swim properly. Eager hands reached down to pull him aboard.

Then they were all staring in silence at the gleaming piece of metal as it lay on the deck. It was gold all right; a Spanish doubloon bearing a cross on one side and a coat of arms on the other – with the date 1714. And it still gleamed as gold as the day it was minted.

After that breathless silence pandemonium broke loose. They were shouting with glee, shaking hands and slapping each other's backs. There really was a treasure wreck down there and they had found it. Suddenly their months of effort, toil, disappointment and sometimes disbelief, were worth it.

But Harry Sherman, the expedition leader, didn't join in their mirth. He was studying the ornament, turning it over in his hand. It was a statuette of some sort, golden like the doubloon, but not at all attractive; in fact, it was downright ugly and evil looking. There was some writing on it. It was not Spanish: Harry recognised the Inca symbols.

He translated very softly; 'Who disturbs me – dies.' But soft though the words were they were heard by the others. Tom went a little pale, but Harry shrugged.

'One doubloon,' he said, 'does not make a fortune. And that wreck has been lost for 250 years. Let's not lose it again in ten minutes. Stacey, down you go with a marker.'

Tom nodded and prepared to dive again. The rest of the crew got busy. They were a lively bunch. There was Big Billy, cook and work-horse of the group, Carlos the Mexican, who knew the waters so well, Phil, Harry's younger brother, and Ron.

In moments, Tom was back in the water, kicking his way to the depths. He should have been up again in less than a minute. After five they guessed he was looking for more gold. After ten they began to scan the surface for him. After fifteen two of the crew donned diving gear and went down to look for him. There was nothing to be seen – not even the marker. Tom had disappeared completely.

The two surfaced and two others went down to search further afield. But they all knew it must be too late. And they all guessed that there was only one way a man could disappear so quickly and so completely. Sharks!

The water teemed with the brutes. Phil shuddered. Carlos picked up the statuette and again read the words. 'Who disturbs me – dies.' He dropped it as if it were a hot coal.

'Drop a marker buoy,' said Harry, 'let's get out of here.' They up-anchored and headed for the coast. The treasure had lost its lustre for the moment.

It was three days before they put to sea again. In future, they had decided, they would dive in pairs. There was a better chance of warding off sharks, that way. Even in the face of death they had decided to carry on.

The *Lucky Star,* a powerful vessel, ploughed through the calm sea, water creaming from her bows. Soon they would round that clump of tropical islands away to the right, and then be in sight of their treasure site.

There was eager anticipation in the air. The sea was as calm as a mill-pond and the weather forecast assured them it was going to stay calm. With no wind to whip up sand and mud, the water would stay clear. Just the job for searching, and with the position of the wreck now known they must be within an inch of success . . .

If only they had known.

In less than half an hour *Lucky Star* had eaten up the miles and brought them into view of the treasure area. And there with a shock they saw a ship, at anchor over their site!

At first they were too amazed to do more than gasp; then came the oaths. Harry Sherman, tight lipped, ordered full speed. This was nothing less than sheer piracy. Their treasure site had been officially registered with the United States Treasury, who legally own all treasure sites in America and in American water. For just a small fee anyone can have licence to search for a lost treasure without anyone else pushing in. If by chance treasure is discovered a quarter of it must be handed over to the state.

The *Lucky Star* was still over a mile away from the other ship when there came signs of movement. It was up-anchoring and making a run for it.

Harry had the binoculars trained on it. It was an old boat, but he knew the *Lucky Star* could never catch it before it reached the cover of the islands with their dozens of secluded coves and inlets. Anyway, he was more interested in some objects being thrown overboard. Through the glasses he could see they were reddish and white, a bit like chunks of meat. Then he realised with a start that they were chunks of meat! He knew at once what the game was: the meat was to attract sharks and prevent diving.

The foul cunning worked, too. Barely had they reached the site when they noticed the dread black triangular fins cutting through the water and the whites of bellies as great sharks twisted and turned below the surface.

What had started out as a peaceful expedition had now become a grim struggle against the baser nature of man and the uncontrollable nature of the sea. The thought of Tom Stacey's loss still lay heavily with them.

Diving was obviously out of the question that day, and there was nothing else to do except sit it out. At least they could guard the site.

Harry fell to pondering. It was bad enough having their site raided, but how had the secret leaked out?

Back on the coast he had warned the rest of the crew to say nothing about the doubloon and the statuette. Even when they had reported the business about Tom Stacey to the police they had said nothing about the gold – just in case, as Harry had said, they got any trouble of the sort they had just experienced.

Harry looked towards the islands where the other boat had fled. Could they have been seen from there? Even with a powerful telescope, he doubted it, and there was only one explanation to his mind. Someone among the crew had indeed talked, but secretly. There must be a traitor on board. It was a chilling thought, but one he kept to himself for the time being.

Harry set everyone working. It would help to cool them down, he thought. Besides, he felt the equipment could do with another check. There was not a lot of it, but it included black frogman suits, breathing apparatus, cylinders of oxygen and a kind of vacuum cleaner to suck away sand and mud to uncover the coins, relics and ornaments.

The timber of the sunken wreck had long since rotted away. It was a case of simply sifting away at the sea-bed until something turned up. And then from the position of things like the ship's bell, anchor and cannon, deciding which way the ship lay when it sank. Careful calculations could then show the likely position of the treasure room. Turbulent waters invariably scattered even the heaviest of metal objects over the years, but at least it was a starting point.

By nightfall everything had been checked and double checked – with many a rueful look towards the islands. But of the other ship there was no more sign and gradually everything settled down to an uneasy quiet.

Big Billy said he'd sit up on deck for a bit and act as guard. 'And I will guard with you,' Carlos snarled. Harry sighed: so the crew, too, thought that one of them was a traitor. The whole business had become rotten, and so far all for a doubloon and a statuette.

Harry let Carlos and Big Billy go on guard together. Not a bad idea anyway to act in pairs, he thought, for they would all sleep easier for it. But Harry didn't sleep, he lay on his bunk, feeling the *Lucky Star* swaying so very gently in the still, almost breathless air. There wasn't a cloud in the sky and the moon rose full and bright. Harry could see it clear in the middle of a porthole. He stared at it and wondered about the strange markings on it, then suddenly it wasn't there anymore. His first reaction was to wonder what had happened to it, then with a wild cry he leapt up from the bunk. 'The boat's loose,' he yelled, rushing to the deck.

Big Billy, startled, wide-eyed and questioning, was pulling a big kitchen knife from his belt. 'Fell asleep,' he apologised. Carlos, suddenly pointing to the surface, shouted: 'There! What's that?'

'Never mind what it is!' cried Harry. 'Why are we drifting? Phil! Ron!' He turned as the others clattered up behind. 'Check the anchor and lower the auxiliary.'

'It was black and shining,' sobbed Carlos. 'It was coming aboard. It is the curse. We shall all die.'

Harry was about to explode in fury, but a call from Phil had him running aft to look at the anchor chain. It had given way deep down, probably at the anchor itself. There was no sign of how, for the links seemed strong and secure. If one *had* gone it had gone at the lower end – but why? The boat had not been straining at it at all. Had it been tampered with when it was lowered? And what had Carlos seen – if he had seen anything at all?

No one slept any more that night, not even Big Billy. He sensed that Ron and Phil and maybe Harry blamed him. If Carlos *was* the traitor and if he hadn't fallen asleep . . .

At first light, Harry had the others working. It didn't take them long to get back to their original marker buoy. But they wondered if that had been moved to another position.

There was only one way to find out; someone had to put on a frogman's suit and go down. Harry glanced at Carlos, but it obviously wasn't going to be him. If he was the traitor he was certainly putting on a good act.

When he looked at Big Billy, the cook shook his head; something of Carlos had rubbed off on him. Harry shrugged. 'I'll go,' he said. Phil and Ron exchanged sheepish looks – but neither offered to go in Harry's place.

Harry was ready in ten minutes and with hardly a glance at anyone, he dropped over the side of the *Lucky Star* and swam down to the depths. He followed the marker buoy down and then looked around for the anchor they had lost in the night. It wasn't far away. He groped along the small length of chain still attached to it and studied the end link. It had been sawn in half. So much for the curse. And the black shiny thing that Carlos had seen? Harry guessed it had been a man in a frogman's suit. Perhaps about to hole the boat, he reasoned, for merely letting it drift away would not have proved very effective.

Harry made for the surface. He was glad of one thing. There wasn't a traitor on board after all. He didn't actually leave the water as he said his piece to shame everyone back to their senses. Then he added: 'We'll search the sea-bed in pairs as we agreed, and we'll keep a watch for whoever's trying to take our treasure from us. Right. You put on a suit, Billy, and follow me down. Carlos, Ron, get the vacuum machine ready to lower down. Phil's got the best eyesight – he'll take first watch.'

Then Harry was gone. The sun was beginning to get up and more light was filtering through to the depths. At last they could take up where Tom Stacey had left off.

Harry began to inch his way across the sea-bed picking away at every little barnacle-encrusted shape that offered itself. Mostly they were just bits of rock, but silver and porcelain, unlike gold, blackened with time and only revealed themselves to be what they were when scrutinised.

Within minutes a shape glided towards him. Harry glanced up and noted the expert way the frogman approached, powerful strokes of the feet, economy of movement of the hands, head well down, reminiscent of the style of Tom. Tom! Tom! It was Tom Stacey! And he had a knife. Harry twisted up and away. But he was awkwardly placed and Stacey was moving in fast. He slashed with the knife, ripping Harry across the thigh.

Blood burst into the water in a cloud as Harry kicked away, but Stacey kicked, too, lunged in with the knife again. Harry grabbed the wrist and the two closed in a desperate struggle.

Suddenly there was a flurry of movement, a dark shadow, a flash of white – and Stacey broke away, his face a mask of fear. But too late, the shark tore in and seized him across the body. Harry felt strong hands at his shoulders. It was Big Billy, and together they made for the surface. There was nothing else they could do.

They got their gold in the end. Twelve hundred coins of gold and two thousand of silver, worth a king's ransom to collectors and to museum keepers the world over. Enough there for all the crew to share. But Stacey, on that day he had made his first discovery, had got the greed of a maniac and on the spur of the moment during his second dive, developed a wild plan to keep everything for himself.

It was Carlos who had the last word: 'It did come true,' he said, 'the curse.'

Hurricane Saddle

Fresh out of college, Dale Fletcher reckoned he'd got the makings of a top bronco-buster. Burdett, the rodeo promoter, was ready to give Dale a real chance to prove himself.

Unfortunately, Burdett put the youngster into the care of a man who was willing to use treachery to gain his own end and unknowingly Dale was heading towards bitter failure.

Young Dale Fletcher hitched his belt higher and moistened dry lips as he climbed the chute rails to straddle the chunky jet-black quarter horse. Looking across the brown dust of the arena to the crowded stands, he did not feel much like junior champion; college rodeo was okay, he guessed, but this had a different feel to it. Now he was competing with real pros.

He wiped sweating hands on his levis. This was his big chance. More than anything else, Dale wanted to sign on with Burdett's circuit. If he made a good showing today. . . .

The announcer's magnified voice cut into his thoughts: 'Dale Fletcher, coming out of chute number two on Black Devil!'

Dale tightened up inside, forced himself to relax. This was the bare-back ride, without saddle or rein, the horse completely uncontrolled. His knees clamped Black Devil's flanks. His left hand gripped the brief leather handhold of the rigging.

Suddenly the chute gate was flung wide and his bronc rocketed out. He remembered the rules: the rider must come out spurring, one hand held away from the horse, and he must stay aboard for eight seconds. Eight seconds on the hurricane deck of a bucking bronco – the longest eight seconds in the world.

Black Devil left the ground in a wild twisting leap, and Dale leant far out to balance himself. Hoofs hit the ground in a bone-jarring thud, sending dust swirling up his nostrils. Black Devil leapt again, shrilling savagely, and Dale felt a mighty wrench at his left arm as he hauled on the strap to stay aboard. He bit his lip and blood ran down his chin as the horse landed stiff-legged.

Black Devil sun-fished, twisting its body in mid-air, as Dale kept his spurs raking. His vision blurred at each hammer blow, till he saw only the black wild-flowing mane before him and heard but dimly the roar of the crowd.

One part of his mind said he was still aboard and that the worst was over; a bronc's strongest bucks came in the first two or three seconds. But Black Devil seemed out to dispute this. He jumped as if he were built of steel springs. Up-twist-down. Up again. . . .

Dale used his free arm to keep balance, used his spurs, spat out blood and dust. His knees clamped hard into the horse's sides as his head jerked back. He yelled out, feeling every jar, riding, riding. . . .

Somewhere a whistle shrilled. His eight seconds had ended. Two pick-up men closed in to hold Black Devil as Dale slid to the ground and walked unsteadily back to the rails.

Dale forced a grin as he climbed over. Willing hands helped him. He saw Burdett looking at him and he forced himself to walk straighter.

The rodeo promoter's voice was casual. 'A good ride, kid – likely you'll pick up some prize money. Doubt if anyone'll better that.'

Dale flushed with pleasure. 'Mister Burdett, sir – I've finished with the junior league, and sure would like to join your circuit.'

Burdett's lanky frame stiffened and he lost his smile. Sharp eyes speared Dale. 'I bet you would! Seems every college kid reckons he can join my outfit, just like that. I'm telling you you need more than one good ride to convince me!'

'Yeah, there's too much luck attached to bare-back riding to prove a man's skill. . . .'

Dale turned to the speaker, beside Burdett; a short bow-legged man wearing a silver-banded Stetson.

'Chet Worth,' Burdett introduced. 'My top bronco-buster.'

'Nice to meet you, Chet,' Dale said, 'and I'm signed up for the saddle-bronc ride.'

Burdett nodded. 'I'll be watching, son. Look after him, Chet.'

'Sure thing, Mr Burdett.' Chet gripped Dale's arm and grinned. 'Come on, kid. Let's find out what horse you've drawn, then maybe I can give you a bit of advice.'

'Gee, thanks, Chet.'

They paused on their way to the chutes watching the calf ropers at work in the arena. A cowboy tossed his lariat and looped the running calf, dismounted and threw it, tied its legs with pigging string.

'Twelve seconds,' Chet calculated. 'Not bad.'

The next event was steer-wrestling. Chet touched Dale's arm and said: 'Watch this – it's Earl Rogers, a real old-timer. You're likely to see a slick piece of work here.'

Dale glanced towards the barrier, where Rogers and his hazer waited. The longhorned steer ran out of the chute, releasing the barrier. Instantly, Roger's hazer began to herd the animal towards the steer wrestler.

Rogers took his chance without hesitation. He left the saddle in a flying leap, gripped the steer's horns in both hands and dug his high heels into the dirt. Then with a powerful heave, he wrestled the steer over on its side and held it pinioned to the ground.

'Yeah,' Chet said admiringly. 'Real slick – only seven seconds. You savvy that 'dogging' – jamming a steer's horn into the turf – isn't allowed these days, kid?'

'I know the rules,' Dale said, a little stiffly. Heck, he was junior champion, wasn't he? This Chet seemed to think he knew nothing.

'Waal, let's take a look at your horse,' Chet said. 'I'm on after you – the bull-ride.'

Chet spoke to one of the judges. 'What's Fletcher riding?'

'Dynamite.'

'I know that one,' Chet said to Dale. 'Pitches with his head low, so you'll need a long rein. Come on, I'll mark your handhold for you.'

Chet strapped a plain saddle on Dynamite's back, and Dale climbed on and slid his feet into the stirrups. He held the single rope rein where Chet had marked it, not to control the horse, but to balance himself.

The announcer's voice boomed across the arena: 'Next rider is Dale Fletcher, who made that fine ride on Black Devil. Out of chute two on Dynamite!'

Dale took a deep breath and nodded for the gate to be opened. Dynamite plunged forward – and with his first buck, Dale knew that something had gone wrong.

Every breath was a torture as the horse bucked and crashed down again and again

Dynamite took off with a high head toss, and the long rein in Dale's hand was immediately useless. He grabbed for a new and shorter handhold as Dynamite pitched and bucked, lifting him clear of the saddle and almost throwing him.

Chet must have known, Dale thought grimly . . . and caught a glimpse of Chet's grinning face above the rail. Then dust swirled in his face and his ears rang as Dynamite hit the ground and bounded up again. Chet had tricked him deliberately, but why?

Dale fought for balance as the crowd roared: 'Ride 'im, cowboy!' Dynamite's head came back, snapping, as he tried to toss his rider.

It was as much as Dale could do to stay aboard. Sweat blinded him. His stomach jolted. Every breath was a torture as the horse bucked and crashed down again and again. . . .

His spurs sawed air instead of Dynamite . . . and the seconds ticked past. He lost count of the jumps. Surely his time must be up? The whistle sounded faint, far-off, and then he saw the pick-up men cutting in towards him.

The announcer's voice came after a pause: 'A disappointing ride by Fletcher. The judges have marked his score low for failing to spur. Hard luck, Dale!'

Dale wiped sweat and dust from his face as he climbed the rails. He knew it had been a poor ride, and felt low. Anger touched him; it wouldn't have been a poor ride if Chet hadn't cheated on the rope.

He saw Burdett looking critically at him. 'I guess you're not ready, son,' the promoter said. 'See me next year, maybe.' And he turned away.

Chet was grinning. 'Too bad, kid,' he drawled, his voice so low as to be almost lost. 'But maybe an old-timer like me doesn't want a youngster stealing his job. Savvy?'

So that was why . . . Dale felt like storming after Burdett and telling him. But would his word be taken against Chet Worth's? Burdett might think he was just making an excuse. . . .

He stared after Chet as the rider waddled towards the chutes.

'Last event of the day, folks,' the announcer boomed. 'The bull ride . . . Chet Worth riding.'

Dale would have left, the rodeo held no further interest for him, but the crowd pressed tighter against the rails for the most spectacular event of all. And Dale found himself penned in.

As the chute gates opened, he found his gaze drawn automatically to the hump-backed bull storming into the open, snorting at the man astride its tawny-grey back, his only hold a loose rope looped round the great body behind the forelegs.

The Brahman bull kicked high with its back legs; then hooked its head round to try to reach Chet with its horns.

Across the arena Dale glimpsed the rodeo clown – the safety man – in skullcap and make-up, and his steel drum padded with rubber tyres. His job was to divert the bull's attention if the rider were thrown.

The crowd was yelling itself hoarse and Chet clung grimly to the humped back of his rampaging two-thousand pound Brahman. The bull pitched madly around the arena, throwing up a smoke screen of choking dust, trying to unseat its rider to get at him with its wicked black horns.

And still Chet rode the cyclone. . . . Dale found himself cheering along with the crowd. It took more than ordinary courage to risk a toss and the pounding hoofs and goring horns.

'Ride 'im, Chet! Ride 'im!'

Still the big Brahman snorted its fury and charged round the arena. Then disaster came. It must have been close to the last of the eight seconds Chet had to stay aboard, and Dale did not quite see how it happened.

One moment, the Brahman was rushing headlong at the rails where he sat, with Chet leaning back for balance; the next moment, Chet went sailing through the air, tossed high above the bull's horns.

A gasp of horror went up from the crowd.

Dale saw Chet hit the dirt and roll over. He fell limp, and appeared to be hurt. The bull did not stop its charge; it lowered its horns and bellowed as it rushed in for the kill.

And the rodeo clown, running across the arena, was too far off. Dale saw that he'd never make it in time to help Chet.

Dale did not hesitate. He vaulted the rail and gauged his distance. He came down towards the Brahman's head, hands grasping for the horns. As his grip tightened on the bony horns, he dug his heels in and used all his strength to wrench the great head down.

This was no contest where pegging was not allowed; he had to save a man's life and there was only one way to do it. He leaned down hard, thrusting one sharp horn into the ground.

The jammed horn acted as a pivot and the bull twisted, bellowing, and crashed over.

Dale rolled clear, jumped up and ran to Chet, dragging him towards the rails. Willing hands reached down from the other side.

Only then did Dale spare a backward glance to see what the bull was doing. He sighed with relief as he saw that the clown had gone into his act, luring the

Brahman away from them. . . .

Safe beyond the rail, Chet turned to Dale. His face was white and set, and he shot a hand out.

'Thanks, kid. Reckon you saved me from a trampling there.'

'He sure did, Chet – and it was as nice a piece of steer-wrestling as I've seen.' Burdett had joined them. 'And say, Fletcher, I guess I can always find a place in my circuit for a plucky youngster. What do you say, Chet?'

Chet Worth grinned broadly. 'I say, yes! Anyway, he'd have made it before if I hadn't given him the wrong buzz on that rope. I'm real sorry now.'

Burdett looked searchingly at Chet. 'Like that, was it, Chet? You durned fool, how many more times have I got to tell you there's always a job for you. Rodeo's a young man's game. Now, reckon you can teach him that little bit extra to make him a top rider?'

'Reckon I can – and will!'

And Dale Fletcher gripped Chet's outstretched hand.

Shadow of the Guillotine

'See that room up there?' leered the surly kitchen-boy to Robert. 'Know who's captive there, citizen? The Comte de Chantelles! No more than a kid but another head for the guillotine.'

Robert glanced up at the top-floor window, then at three soldiers of the National Guard lounging outside the house. Rescuing the young count from a blood-chilling death was not going to prove an easy task.

From the attic high above the Paris streets the English boy contemplated the roof of the building opposite. He knew exactly where the skylight was and how he was going to reach it. Once inside the house he must act according to circumstances.

His gaze dropped to a top-floor window where a light burned behind drawn curtains. Within that room was a prisoner of the Revolution, the young Comte de Chantelles.

And from the dark street below rose the voice of the Paris mob celebrating the second anniversary of the Bastille's fall. It was two years since that fateful July day of 1789, years during which the tide of revolution had swept over France engulfing innocent and guilty alike. To be an aristrocrat was to be doomed.

Among those to die had been Baston Malnay, Comte de Chantelles, but not before he had seen his wife and family safely into hiding.

Three months ago arrangements were completed for their escape to England. But the plan had been only partly successful, for although the Comtesse and her two small daughters had been smuggled out of France, a last-minute betrayal had delivered the young Comte into the hands of his enemies.

In three days' time he would go to the guillotine.

Unless . . .

The English boy frowned. Escape from France was not easy. Even the King had failed. Just over a month ago the Royal Family had been seized at Varennes and brought back to Paris where they were now virtually prisoners of their own subjects. And the city was rife with wild rumours. With men like Robespierre in command, anything could happen . . . even to a king.

But Robert Deauville Fleming was not concerned with the broader issues. Only with his mission: to rescue the young Comte de Chantelles.

Robert had for long known that his elder brother was engaged in the dangerous work of snatching intended victims from the guillotine, but when he had claimed the right to assist in this work, Paul had refused.

'Sixteen is too young an age, brother. Perhaps when you are older and – heaven forbid – if such employment is still necessary . . .'

Robert, however, had taken matters into his own hands.

When Paul had next left London he had followed him to the coast and sneaked aboard the sloop his brother had joined. During the brief cross-Channel voyage he had remained hidden, swimming ashore when a rowing boat had landed Paul on French soil under cover of night. Only when the sloop had put about did he reveal himself, by which time it was too late for Paul to do other than accept his presence philosophically.

'No doubt we can make use of you,' he had said wryly. 'Thanks to our maternal *grandmère* you speak the language well enough, and know your Paris. But this is no youth's lark – there are prizes on the heads of such as we. Take care at all times.'

Within half an hour Robert had good reason to recall his brother's warning, for only by the skin of their teeth did they evade a patrol of the National Guard, and only then at the cost of a broken ankle for Paul.

There Paul had told him, 'Fate would seem to have decreed you shall act alone in this matter. Here are your orders . . .'

Quitting the attic, Robert descended to the street where the noise of the marching, chanting mob was almost deafening. Many of the marchers carried torches, others bore effigies, including one of the King.

Outside the house where the young Comte was held captive lounged three soldiers of the National Guard. Robert glanced idly up to the top-floor window. That the young Comte was held in that very room he had ascertained from a surly youth employed in the house as a kitchen-boy. Pierre Lumel was coarse of manner and speech.

'Come to Paris to see the aristos die, eh?' he had leered at Robert. 'Well, there's one I know is due to die any day now! See that room, citizen? Yes, that one. Know who's captive there? The Comte de Chantelles! No more than a kid, but still acting like he was a 'somebody' instead of just another head for the guillotine! These aristos!'

Robert had concealed his satisfaction. Paul had given him the address to watch. Now he knew the very room. And before long he had gleaned from the spiteful Lumel the vital information that the prisoner was served a meal at ten o'clock each night.

It needed but thirty minutes to that hour.

Elbowing through the procession to the far pavement Robert sauntered past the guarded house and the mouth of an alley where two more soldiers were posted. Beyond was a baker's shop – its windows boarded – and another alley into which he turned. Here he boldly entered a doorway and climbed stairs leading to apartments above the shop. On the second floor landing a man and a woman emerged suddenly from one of the rooms but they gave him no more than a casual glance as they hurried down to the street.

On the deserted top floor he heaved himself on to the roof through the skylight. Over the Paris rooftops he could see torchlight processions converging upon the Place de la Bastille. At a crouch he moved to where he could see the soldiers guarding the alley; they were busy exchanging shouts with the marchers.

He judged the distance to the far building – and jumped.

It seemed the clatter he made on landing must surely be heard, but no alarm was raised. He advanced cautiously along the sloping roof to the skylight he had selected for his entry. Noiselessly he raised it. There was a crude wooden ladder, and after a moment of listening he started down.

The ladder finished in a tiny alcove off a passage dimly lit by a single flickering lamp, and with stairs at the far end. He counted off the doors of the rooms overlooking the street. Behind the third of these the young Comte was held prisoner. But there was nothing he could do – yet.

Pierre Lumel had boasted the door was kept locked at all times and even from here he could see there was no key in the lock. He must bide his time, be ready to strike when the moment came.

The minutes dragged. From outside the house came the muffled tramp of the mob. Once, from below, he caught the sound of voices and raucous laughter.

Then – suddenly, it seemed – footsteps clumped on the stairs. Robert tensed.

The soldier who appeared was sloppily dressed in an ill-fitting uniform. His musket was slung over one shoulder and he carried a tray of food and drink. At the third door he halted, produced a key, used it in the lock and entered the room.

Robert moved swiftly and silently. The soldier was apologising, in a voice filled with mockery, for the poor quality of the meal he had brought. Robert peered round the half-open door. The soldier stood with his back to it. Facing him was a slightly built, dark-haired boy of fourteen or fifteen whose quiet dignity now goaded his tormentor to lurid threats.

'Eat it, I say! Eat it, Monsieur le Comte, before I thrust your noble face in it! The mob wants a fat neck for the guillotine!'

Robert inched round the door, finger to his lips in warning. Only by a flicker of his eyelids did the young Comte betray his surprise; then, to hold the soldier's attention he began begging the man to help him.

Robert's hand closed over a small but heavy statuette on a table just inside the door. The ideal weapon.

Too late the soldier sensed danger. As he whirled, unslinging his musket, Robert struck, catching the man as he slumped unconscious and dumping him in a chair. Then he turned to the young Comte de Chantelles.

'Follow me, quickly!' he said urgently in French.

The passage was deserted. Quickly he led the boy to the alcove and up to the roof.

Five minutes later they were mingling with the Paris mob.

From where they lay in the woods the two youngsters watched the soldiers ride from sight. Then, as the drumming of hoofs died on the still evening air, they exchanged grins. It was almost forty-eight hours since their dramatic meeting, and in that time they had become staunch friends.

Slipping out of Paris had been easy enough on that night of celebration, and throughout the hours of darkness they had covered many kilometres of their journey to the coast. But with the coming of dawn they had lain low, as Paul had impressed upon Robert they must. For the alarm would have been raised.

Eagle-eyed revolutionaries would be everywhere watching for the young Comte who had cheated the guillotine.

So they had holed up, moving again only with the return of nightfall. Once more, at daybreak, they had gone to ground. Now they were impatient for the evening shadows to fold about them yet again.

Food was their immediate need but Robert knew that this night should see their hunger satisfied. Only a few kilometres distant, close by the village of Vereux, was the farm of Gervais Charpentier. There, Paul had told him, they would find not only food but shelter; and – with luck – transport for the rest of the journey.

Dusk was deepening when finally they stirred, and by the time they first saw the river the moon had risen. Beyond a humped stone bridge were the closely clustered buildings of Vereux.

'We must use the bridge,' Robert told his companion. 'Once across it we can slip round the village to the farm of Monsieur Charpentier.'

They were almost across the bridge when the unexpected happened. A soldier stepped into their path at the far end and from behind his musket called upon them to stop. 'Leave the talking to me,' Robert whispered urgently as they obeyed the command.

The soldier advanced.

'Who are you?' he demanded. 'What is your business?'

Robert decided to try bluff.

'Good evening, citizen,' he replied cheerfully in French. 'You startled us! As for who we are, I am Dominique Marin and this is my brother Charles. Our business is delivering a message from our father to our Uncle François.' He pointed downstream to a lone cottage he had noticed earlier. 'Do you not remember us?'

'That's hardly likely,' grunted the soldier, 'seeing my company only moved in this afternoon.'

'Is something afoot then?' Robert enquired eagerly.

'Who knows? All I do is obey orders.'

Lowering his musket the sentry gestured they should continue and walked with them to the end of the bridge. But even as Robert complimented himself on the success of his bluff two more uniformed figures bore down upon them. One, a sergeant, barked, 'What goes on? Who are these two?'

'Lads visiting their uncle,' mumbled the soldier.

'Lads?' The sergeant peered suspiciously at Robert, then at the young Comte. His close-set eyes widened with immediate recognition. Simultaneously, as his hand whipped out and closed round the boy's arm with a grip of steel, he rasped at the others to seize Robert.

Resistance was futile. The sergeant glowered at the sentry.

'For your information, blockhead, *this* lad is the Comte de Chantelles – and the other is the scoundrel who made possible his escape!'

His gaze returned malevolently to the young aristrocrat. 'You will not remember me, Monsieur le Comte, but *I* remember *you* – from the days when I slaved on your father's estate. By the heads of all the aristos in France, this is a night that pleases me!'

Ten minutes later the two boys were locked in a room above the village inn. Outside the door guards were posted. Others watched beneath the window. And the sergeant had already despatched a courier to his superiors in neighbouring Comballe informing them of his apprehension of the Comte de Chantelles.

Very soon, he had promised his young prisoners, they would be travelling the road back to Paris . . . and the guillotine.

Sooner even than Robert had feared the door was flung open and a captain of the National Guard strode in, followed by the sergeant. The officer was young.

'So!' he sneered. ' Our little noble bird is back in the cage! Excellent!' He turned to the sergeant. 'Be sure your vigilance will not go unrewarded. It was fortunate indeed that we ran into your courier on our way here. Have a carriage prepared at once, we will transfer our prize to Comballe without delay.'

'Very good, *mon capitaine,*' the sergeant smiled ingratiatingly. 'If I could accompany you to make my own report . . .?'

'Why not? After all, the glory is yours.'

The two men left together. Then, in no time at all it seemed, the young prisoners were being hustled from the inn to a waiting coach. When the captain and sergeant had climbed in after them, the officer gave an order to move off, and as the coach rolled from the cobbled forecourt Robert saw they had an escort of six mounted soldiers.

Robert's thoughts were glum as the coach lurched through the night. His brother had entrusted him with this mission and he had failed. And because he had failed, a young lad must keep his appointment with the guillotine.

Opposite them the captain sat poker-faced, but clearly the sergeant was savouring his triumph.

'What I wouldn't give,' thought Robert, 'to wipe that smirk off his face!'

They must have covered some eight kilometres when on a sudden shout the coachman dragged his team to a violent halt.

'See what is wrong,' commanded the captain.

At once the sergeant thrust his head through the window – and slumped with a groan as something heavy descended upon it. Simultaneously the coach door was jerked open and he fell into the road.

On his feet, the captain called briskly, 'Tie him up, hide him where he won't quickly be found. Then get moving – and fast!'

Calmly he sat down again, grinned at the bewildered boys.

'Things are not always what they appear to be,' he said casually.

Then, as the coach rolled forward again, he continued in English and addressing a flabbergasted Robert, said:

'We got word from the village you had been captured. I was at the Charpentier farm – your brother thought it advisable I should meet you there. We intercepted the courier, donned these uniforms and – well, you know the rest.'

He settled back in his seat. 'We shall reach the coast before dawn. Your brother will meet us – and so will a sloop.'

It was as the Englishman had promised. On a deserted stretch of beach they were met by Paul and hurried aboard a waiting ship, and when Robert wakened from the deep sleep he had drifted into, it was to see the White Cliffs of Dover bathed in sunshine.

'Now,' he smiled at the French boy by his side, 'you are really safe.'

Paul joined them.

'Your mother and sisters are awaiting you on shore,' he told the young Comte de Chantelles. Then, arching an eyebrow at Robert, he said, 'It seems after all, you weren't too young for our dangerous work. Well done, lad. I'm proud of you.'

The young Comte smiled across at Robert. He, too, felt proud. Proud to have the young Englishman for a friend.

Leave it to the Experts

The beaver was lying quite still in about three feet of water, against the dam. Was it dead? Then Len and Frank spotted the chain of a trap and hauled out the dead beaver. Caught well under-water, the animal had been held there and drowned.

'Someone's getting ready to blow this dam,' said Frank, 'and he's killing the beavers first because if he didn't, the beavers would have the gap plugged up again in a few hours.'

Little did the two friends think at that moment that they were heading for a terrifying adventure.

Sam Goodson, game warden for several hundred square miles of the British Columbia wilderness, was completing his instructions to the two boys. 'Now, you have the map of the area firmly fixed in your minds, I think.'

'Yes,' said Frank, 'It seems pretty simple. We're at the head of the Yukul-kum River. It runs from here roughly south-west for 40 miles until it meets up with the Nakwundo. The whole Yukulkum is really a series of beaver marshes and lakes, full of beaver dams. We just follow them down to the last dam above the river junction, and meet you there in four days.'

'We'll have the river on our right and a strip of forest on our left,' Len took up the recital. 'Beyond that strip are ranches and farms, so if we get into any difficulty we won't be too far from help.'

'That's right,' Sam agreed. 'I'd take you with me down the far side of the river, into the deep forest, but in this drought it's tinder-dry over there and safer on this side. The Yukulkum is wide and wet enough to stop any fire from the other side springing across to here.'

'Anyway, I'll spend the next four days ranging through there, seeing what I can about conditions and wildlife. Your job is to stick to the river and give me a report on water levels, number of beaver lodges, state of the dams and so on. You won't see many beavers, though, unless you hide up at dusk and wait for them to come out. You'll not see a beaver in broad daylight!'

'Yes, sir!' said Frank. 'We've studied beavers in our nature conservancy classes. We'll do a good job, don't you worry.'

The ranger grinned at the eager faces turned towards him. This was paradise for the two boys. Frank was his nephew, and Len was Frank's inseparable pal. For years they'd been after Sam to take them on a tour one summer. Now both were good riders and competent woodsmen. Sam was pleased he'd brought them on this trip. They'd be safe from forest fires *and* bears on this side of the river, it was almost impossible for them to get lost, and at the same time they'd be learning self-reliance during the four days on their own.

If he'd known what was going to happen in those four days Sam wouldn't have been looking so pleased as he swung into his saddle, gathered up the lead of his pack horse and trotted off, waving a lazy goodbye. In fact, he probably wouldn't have left them on their own at all.

Frank and Len watched until Sam was out of sight among the trees, sitting easy and relaxed in the saddle. Then they let out a whoop together.

'Yahoo!' Len cried. 'On our own for four days!'

'Yeah. And cold beans tonight if we don't get moving and find a good camping place before dusk,' Frank retorted.

The boys quickly mounted their horses, Len leading the pack horse carrying their sleeping bags and food supplies. They turned away from the water, through the bordering willow and aspens and on to higher, firmer ground. Here the spruce was tall, and walking the horses between them was easier.

It was almost dark under the trees before they broke out into a sizeable clearing – a sparse, rock-strewn area where they could build a fire safely.

Len unsaddled and hobbled the horses, and left them to graze on the grass near the edge of the clearing. Hobbled horses rarely stray far, and he knew they'd stay in the clearing for the night.

Meanwhile Frank had been into the trees gathering firewood and green jack-pine boughs. By the time Len had finished with the horses Frank had the frying pan over a fire, and chunks of bacon were sizzling appetisingly. When these were done and transferred to tin plates, he emptied a can of baked beans into the pan, stirred them into the fat and quickly heated them. Len found eating irons and some fairly well-preserved bread in the pack and set them out. Both boys were ravenous, and tucked in without ceremony. Conversation ceased until the last scraps were wiped from the plates.

'Marvellous, just what I needed,' Len grunted, making himself more comfortable against a jutting boulder. 'Any apples?'

Frank finished extinguishing the fire with water from a large canteen, then found some apples in the pack and tossed one to Len. 'Don't you ever stop eating?'

'Only when I'm not hungry,' Len retorted. 'Say, this is great, eh, Frank? On our own, and with a proper job, too.'

'Yeah,' said Frank. 'You're not scared?'

'Who, me? Of course not,' Len replied. Then: 'What was *that?*'

The shrill, abruptly stifled scream had brought both boys to their feet. 'Oh,' Frank laughed weakly. 'A rabbit, probably. An owl or a coyote's got him.'

'Gosh, it didn't spook the horses, did it?' Len asked 'It sure got me there for a minute.'

'No, they're more used to forest noises than we are,' said Frank. 'But let's check before we turn in.'

They found the horses calmly grazing, undisturbed by the night noises. Frank was right – they were an experienced lot, specially chosen by Sam for their calm temperaments. The boys checked the hobbles, then turned back to settle themselves for the night.

The springy pine boughs Frank had collected made comfortable mattresses under their sleeping bags. In five minutes the boys' muffled snores were added to the other natural sounds of the night.

Next morning saw them breaking up camp bright and early and heading back towards the beaver marshes. They kept up among the big growth of spruce, fir and jack-pine and made better time than in the boggy, tangled thickets nearer the marshes.

By mid-morning they were round the first marsh, and came rather unexpectedly to its source. Len whistled in surprise at the size of the beaver dam. It was a magnificent edifice, about 50 feet long, a thin stream of water running smoothly over its top along almost the full length.

They dismounted and approached the dam, an intricate construction of twiggy branches and mud. Beyond, in the still waters of the marshy lake, they could see the tops of three beaver lodges. In full light of day there were no beavers about, but a mother teal, alert to their approach, was fussily shepherding her brood away.

'Look, there's the beaver's feed-bed,' said Len, pointing to an untidy mass of aspen twigs and branches, mostly stripped of their bark, in the shallow water at the lake's edge. Scrambling through the tangled willows and aspens they finally managed to get within a few feet of the feed-bed. There they found plenty of beaver tracks, and a few smaller, more delicate foot-prints.

'Mink,' said Frank. 'The mother beavers around here had better keep a sharp lookout, or they'll be losing a few kits to that fellow. Mink are always hanging about hoping to pick off a young one if they get their chance.'

Before moving on they took a good look round, noting the number of lodges and making other remarks on the dam and lake in their notebooks.

Apart from the second night, when they could find no suitable site for a campfire and so had to eat cold beans, the next three days were uneventful. The morning of the fourth day found them approaching the second-last dam in the chain.

'We're in good time,' Frank said. 'We'll be at the last dam by early afternoon. Wonder who gets there first, Sam or us?'

Len scrambled ahead and was standing on the dam, pointing, when Frank sauntered up. 'Something wrong here,' Len said.

'What?' Frank was beside Len quickly, peering into the water. 'Why, that's a beaver!'

The animal was lying quite still in about three feet of water, against the dam. Was it dead? Then they spotted the chain of a trap and hauled out the dead beaver. Caught well under-water, the beaver had been held there and drowned.

The startled boys examined the rest of the dam, finding five more traps, three of which held limp bodies. They hauled out and sprang the empty traps, placing the whole 'catch' on top of the dam.

'Why should anyone be trapping beaver in high summer?' Len asked. 'The pelts are too thin to sell for fur, and no one eats beaver meat, do they?'

'No.' Frank was very angry. 'Whoever has the trapping rights on this territory hasn't done this. The only thing I can think of is that someone's getting ready to blow this dam.'

'Dynamite it? Why?'

'You know the farmers near here get their irrigation water from the beaver lakes. You've seen their ditches leading off through the woods from the lakes.'

'Sure, and most of them were pretty dry, too. But why kill the beavers before blowing the dam?'

'Because,' said Frank, 'the beavers would have the gap plugged up again in a few hours, no matter how big it was. I'll bet you if we go downstream we'll find that some farmer has a ditch running from the lowest lake, but the lake's too low and his ditch isn't getting any water.'

'You mean he plans to drain this lake into the lower one, and fill it up so that the water will run into his ditch again?'

'Yep. Let's go see.'

They hurried downstream as fast as their horses could push through the tangled aspen and willow. Where the stream began widening into the lowest lake, they found a dry ditch.

'Hmmm. Right so far,' said Frank. 'You see how the drought's made the lake shrink quite a lot, so the water doesn't reach this ditch any more. Tell you what we'd better do,' he decided. 'You go down to the lower dam and wait for Sam. Bring him straight back to where we found the traps. I'll go back there and stop the trapper if he tries anything. Hurry up, he might be going to blow it today!'

Len pushed off downstream and Frank kicked his horse to a trot, heading back for the endangered dam.

All appeared peaceful as he approached it. He tied up his horse and strode out on to the dam. If anyone wanted to try any funny business, they'd have him to deal with first!

He had barely taken three strides on to the dam when a man burst from the trees on the opposite bank, shouting and waving wildly, running towards the dam.

Startled, Frank stood stockstill. The man continued towards him, was well on to the dam before Frank understood his words.

'Get off, kid! Get off! It's going to blow any minute!' The man was shouting frantically, waving him back.

That was warning enough for Frank. He bolted, and had just reached firm ground when the blast hit him. He was thrown forward and down, along with clods of mud, water, branches and rocks, by the indiscriminate blast. He lay still.

Len had just reached the lower dam and had seen that Sam hadn't yet arrived when he heard the blast. He ran to his horse, paused, then shot back to the dam where he threw down his red neckerchief. On it he arranged three sticks in an arrow pointing upstream. That would be clue enough for Sam when he turned up. Then, the detour having taken no more than 20 seconds, Len ran back to his horse, vaulted into the saddle, and headed upstream fast.

Careless of whipping branches that tore at his clothes, and uneven footing that could bring him and horse down in a nasty fall, Len drove ahead as fast as the horse would move. And that wasn't a slow pace, either. Len's haste was communicated to the horse, who laid back his ears and galloped, his hooves finding the safe ground surely as he wove in and out of the trees.

Around the lower lake they tore. As they reached the stream below the blown dam, Len saw that it was boiling down at a terrific pace. Sure enough, the dam above had gone! Then he came in sight of the dam, saw a great breach in its centre and a torrent of water as the whole lake above tried to throw itself through.

He didn't see Frank at first. Then, as he pulled up his sweating horse, he saw his friend, lying flat on his face, spattered with mud, a branch lying across his back.

'Frank!' Even as Len cried out, he saw Frank stir, move an arm. 'Thank God!'

He knelt beside Frank, removed the branch. Frank groaned, then sat up slowly.

'No bones busted, but I feel as if I've got some gorgeous bruises on my back. What about the man?'

'What man?' Len looked about. There was no one else in sight.

Frank explained. 'He must have been a lot closer to the blast than I was. He ran right into it to warn me!'

They climbed on to the tattered remains of the dam, searching for any sign of the man. 'That was a darned brave thing to do,' said Frank miserably. 'We'd better look downstream. He might have been carried away.'

'No, there he is!' Len shouted, pointing excitedly. The man lay inside the dam, half in the water, his back and shoulders against the dam, the current pulling at his legs.

The boys stared helplessly. The unconscious man – he might be dead – was on the far side of the breach. Twenty feet of raging water separated them. As they watched aghast the figure slipped a little, dropped an inch or two deeper into the water. The hungry current pulled at him.

'*We* – we *can't* leave him there. But if we try going round, he'll be sucked away before . . .' Frank dithered, his usual decisive manner completely gone.

Len looked curiously at his friend. That must have been quite a knock to leave Frank wavering like this. It was usually Frank who took the lead in everything, with Len following. Now it was up to Len!

'Only one thing,' he snapped decisively. 'I'll swim out to him.' Then, as Frank began to protest: 'With a horse. There's no time to try anything else.'

'You'll have to help,' he told the still-dazed Frank, thrusting a coiled rope into his hands. 'We'll tie this to the saddle pommels on each horse. You back off along the bank upstream, till there's a tight rope between the horses. Then as I go into the water, move with us, keeping the rope tight. You'll be our anchor, and keep us from being washed through the gap. Hurry up!'

Frank obediently climbed on to his horse. He followed his part of the manoeuvre carefully, keeping the rope taut, and moving slowly towards the dam as Len's horse waded into the water.

Len's stomach jolted unpleasantly as his horse, having hesitated momentarily, began swimming. He felt the water crawl up past his knees, but the horse's back stayed clear and he struck out determinedly, fighting the current that tried to sweep them towards the breach.

How they managed to avoid all the underwater tangles of branches accumulated around the dam by generations of hard-working beavers is a mystery. But with Frank keeping a tight rope between, Len reached the man in a surprisingly short time.

It was then that Len realised he had no plan to get the man back! There wasn't any time for niceties. The hungry current was pulling hard, the man was in up to his shoulders now! The snorting horse was thrashing and jinking.

'Steady, boy, we'll head back in a minute,' Len soothed. Then, loosening the second rope he'd brought, he leaned down until he was almost toppling from the saddle, and managed to get the rope under the man's shoulders. Knotting it quickly but securely, he hitched it up as high as he could, pulling it round the pommel. The man came free from the dam and floated alongside the horse, his head barely clear of the water. Len signalled and Frank began backing off. Len had to lean to the opposite side of the saddle to balance the weight as they struggled back. If the man's head went under, it was a risk they had to take.

The return trip was fast, with Len's horse urged by the pulling rope. He stopped as his hooves bit into the bank, the man's limp weight holding him back. The boys quickly pulled the man clear of the water.

'Is he alive?' Frank asked.

'Dunno. Haven't had time to look.'

The question was answered by the man himself, who abruptly sat up, muttering: 'The kid on the dam. Is he . . .?'

'Right here, mister. You all right?' Frank answered, but the man had slumped back again.

It was Sam, who rode up fast on a sweating horse just then, who rapidly took in the situation and knelt beside the man, holding the limp wrist to feel for a pulse. He lifted an eyelid, examined the turned-up eyeball. 'Fainted. Shock, probably.' Then, turning to the boys: 'Blankets and a fire!'

The exhausted boys hurried to do his bidding, then both crowded close to the flames, shivering.

'Hmmmm. Had quite an adventure, I see, but I think you'll survive,' Sam said, turning from the man's blanket-wrapped figure. 'Reckon he'll be all right, too. No bones broken. Now, what happened?'

Sam whistled when the boys finished their story. 'What an idiot! But brave, too. Nearly killed himself to warn you, Frank.'

Half an hour later the man had recovered, and after gratefully swallowing a tin mug of hot soup, told his part of the story. His name was Crombie, and he'd just bought the nearby farm, having moved to British Columbia from southern Ontario, which he found too tame and overcrowded for his taste.

'Well, this ought to be enough excitement to last you for a while,' Sam remarked dryly. 'Didn't anyone tell you, though, what a fool trick it is to break up the beaver dams? Those beavers are your best friends! If you didn't have them here, building their dams and holding back all this water, you'd never have any water in the summers. The spring melt would just gush straight down the Yukulkum. Then you *would* be in a pickle. Wouldn't be able to grow a thing.'

'Yeah,' Crombie protested weakly, 'but my crops were dying in this drought. What else could I do?'

'Like everybody else round here,' replied Sam promptly. 'Either dig your ditch further to reach the water again, or invest in a pump and hose. The beavers can afford to let you have some water, but not the lot!'

'Never thought of that,' muttered Crombie sitting up. 'Guess I'm in trouble now, eh?'

'Well, trapping beaver out of season is an offence. So's blowing up dams, any season,' Sam replied.

'But we'll speak up for you,' Frank put in. 'You saved my life. Nearly killed yourself doing it.'

'I'm not exactly ungrateful, myself,' said Crombie. 'I'd have been a goner without you boys to pull me out.'

'Now then,' said Sam, who'd wandered off to draw some water and was busy pouring it over the fire, 'if you lot are recovered well enough to do all that jawing, you're well enough to do a bit more travelling. We can make it to Haverstown by late afternoon.'

'Gosh, you're in a hurry,' Len remarked.

'Sure am. Guess I'll go have to catch me a few live beaver to put in this lake. Somebody's got to repair that dam, and we might as well leave it to the experts!'

The Double Agent

The Head of MI5 looked steadily at his most trusted agent.

'We have a double agent in our midst,' he said suddenly. 'During the last six months a number of our European contact men have either disappeared or met with fatal accidents. One of you lot has been passing on their identity and whereabouts to the enemy. He must be stopped – dead!'

The nightmare began one late September afternoon. It was raining and there was already an autumn chill in the air that bored through my raincoat and into my bones. I don't suppose it was really all that cold, but I hadn't been well for some time, and I was sensitive to any changes of temperature. I was on my way to J.J.'s house in Hampstead on the edge of the Heath, a pleasant enough spot on a nice day, but depressing in the rain with the sodden leaves lying thick in the gutters to remind one that another summer had passed that could never be recalled. All in all, it was an afternoon that was in keeping with my mood, which was near suicidal, owing to the fact that J.J. had asked me to see him.

J.J. is a civil servant, in a manner of speaking, though a very unofficial one. To put it in plain words, J.J. is the Head of MI5. He is also my boss.

To destroy a few myths about our game, I should tell you first of all that J.J. operates entirely from his house on the Heath, and not from behind the facade of some fancy front such as the Greengrocer's Marketing Board, or the Levant Importer's Offices, as some of these fiction writers would have you believe. The set-up, in fact, is a very simple one. J.J., who looks like an irritable solicitor, sits there all day with his mouse-like secretary, sifting through Intelligence reports, and occasionally dictating a few letters, which are quickly lost in someone else's files. When something does blow up, he phones one of his agents and a meeting is arranged. These meetings generally lead to mayhem and murder in some distant European capital. I was on my way to such a meeting.

In actual fact it wasn't the prospect of some future unknown danger that was worrying me that afternoon. What *was* worrying me was that I had been on a great many operations and I knew that I was beginning to crack. On top of it all I had been having frequent black-outs, which went on for several hours, and even lasted a whole day or night, sometimes, and I was wondering if any of this had got back to J.J. somehow, and that I had been summoned to be given the chop.

J.J. lives in a rambling Victorian house which needs a good coat of paint. On that particular afternoon, with the green mould on its walls glistening with the rain, it looked positively sinister. The door was opened by his secretary who was wearing a cardigan that reeked of moth balls. Without a word she led me into a room where J.J. was sitting at his desk, with the usual litter of papers in front of him. He hardly looked at me as I came into the room.

'Take a chair.'

I sat down in the chair he indicated and waited while he fiddled with some of his papers. In a corner of the room a grandfather clock heaved itself into action and struck four in doom-laden tones.

'Double agents,' J.J. said irritably, looking up at last. 'They're the curse of this business.' He wagged a thin stick of a finger at me. 'Do you know why they do it?'

'For money?' I said.

'You're too intelligent to really think that,' J.J. said. 'The trouble inevitably begins when an agent starts questioning himself about what he's doing. The next thing you know he's working for the other side as well as for us.' He brooded. 'One can understand it, I suppose. The demarcation line between right and wrong in this business has always been a fine one.'

I waited for him to get to the point. Whatever that point was, it certainly didn't seem to be leading up to a demand for my resignation from the Service. I began to relax.

'We have a double agent in our midst,' J.J. said suddenly. 'I want you to find him.'

'You've picked the best man for the job,' I said.

'I've had my best man working on this for the last two months,' J.J. said. 'Peter Yates.'

The smile slipped from my face. 'I've always worked alone,' I said sulkily.

'You're working alone on this one,' J.J. said. 'Yates is dead. Knocked down by a car in a country lane just outside Middlesham. A plain case of murder, if you ask me. Now I'll fill you in on a few details. . . .'

The basic details were straight forward enough. Over the last six months a number of our European contact men who had been very active in the field had either disappeared or met with fatal accidents. Clearly, a list of their names had been supplied to the opposition who had set to work with efficient enthusiasm on a process of elimination. J.J. leaned back tired in his chair. 'Only my little band of men knew their names. So obviously it's one of you lot who has been passing on the information.'

I thought about that for a moment. 'You're sure you can trust *me*, in that case?'

'You've been working for me for a long, long time,' J.J. said. 'If I can't trust you, I can't trust anyone. It's probably one of the new boys. He must be stopped – *dead*!'

I rose to my feet. 'All right. Where do I start?'

'At Middlesham, of course,' J.J. said. 'Where else?'

I was in Middlesham by six-thirty that evening. Middlesham is in Essex, and it is one of those terrible little suburbs that sprung up, full of hope, in the thirties, and never got off the ground. There was still a little light, but it was raining as I came out of the station and wandered a little aimlessly past a derelict cinema, whose ancient posters flapped forlornly in the wind that was whipping down the High Street.

Although I wasn't sure exactly where I was going to start, I knew that my late colleague would only have come to this spot for some very good reason. It followed on from that, that he had probably wandered around, asking a few pertinent questions. The obvious thing for me was to do likewise. I ambled into the nearest pub and quickly got into conversation with the landlord. After the usual dreary pleasantries, I got around to the accident that had occurred the night before. The landlord's manner immediately became a little more lively. 'He was in here, you know,' he said. 'I recognised him at once from the picture they printed of him in the local paper.'

'Yes?' I tried to look casual. 'Did you talk to him?'

'Only for a few minutes.' He picked up a glass and began polishing it. 'He was asking for Three Gables House.'

I stared at the faded photograph of the winning team of a long forgotten cricket match that was on the wall behind the bar. They stared back glassily over the years and I thought: it's too easy. It just doesn't drop into one's lap like this. But I knew that sometimes it did. 'Goodnight,' I said, and I went out into the rain again.

It was Thursday, and some of the shops were still open, including the local newsagent. I went in, the rain dripping off me. 'Three Gables,' I said. 'Do you deliver newspapers there?'

'Mr Armstrong's place?' The newsagent stared at the pool I was making on the floor. 'Yes –we deliver there. What about it?'

'I have to see him,' I said. 'A matter of insurance. Can you tell me how to find the house please?'

Armed with a complicated set of instructions I set off again, walking against the wind, until I finally found myself in the hinterland of Middlesham, where a series of detached houses of the thirties reared up from out of the darkness like abandoned pill boxes. Mr Armstrong's house, when I eventually found it proved to be a pseudo–Tudor affair. I was standing there, thinking that Mr Armstrong had more money than taste, when suddenly I felt the back of my hair beginning to prickle. In our game, if you're lucky, you develop an extra sense about trouble. It is almost as if the brain develops some sort of antennae that can pick up any signal of danger. At that moment my brain was registering something, and I didn't know what it was, but I did know that something was wrong. I began to move forward – very, very slowly.

There were no lights anywhere, and as it was still early it was safe to assume that Mr Armstrong was either away, or not yet home from work. Even so, with the warning signals still registering in my brain, I took my time getting into the house – by the usual expedient of cutting a neat square of glass out of the window.

Inside I stumbled around blindly for a minute or two in the darkness, which was so complete that it was almost suffocating. I had just decided to risk switching on the light, when my foot encountered something soft on the floor. It felt like a cushion. But when I bent down to touch it, I found it wasn't a cushion at all. It was a body.

I found the switch and then went back to examine what I had found. It was a man with a bullet hole through his heart. He was about the same age as myself and dressed in a well-cut and expensive looking suit. I recognised him at once.

His name was Colin Avory, and like myself he was a professional spy, except that he had worked for the other side until he was finally tumbled.

After that he had gone quickly underground, presumably as Mr Armstrong. I stared down at him, laid out there quite neatly on the flowered Wilton carpet. Mr Armstrong, living quietly in Middlesham, no doubt respected, possibly even liked by the tradespeople and those living around him.

In the distance, a clock struck eight, bringing me back sharply to the present. Diving my hand into his pocket, I fished out his wallet and went through it. The first thing I came across was a theatre ticket for a musical show, dated for the next evening. Now there was no reason at all why the dead man shouldn't want to go to the theatre. But what *was* strange was the fact that I also found the used stub of another ticket for the same show, dated for the previous month. In the first place it was a very bad musical, and anyone in his right senses wouldn't want to see it for a second time. What was much more to the point was the fact that both tickets were for the same row and seat number in the Dress Circle. Which, to say the least of it, was quite a coincidence. It didn't need much brain power to work it out. Avory had been using the theatre as a rendezvous for the passing over of information.

Putting the unused ticket into my own wallet, I got down to searching the house, but I found nothing. Switching off the lights, I left the house and went out into the rain again.

Back in town it suddenly occurred to me that as two people had died since we had started prying into the matter, it might be best if I let J.J. know what had happened so far, just in case I went the same way. I went into the nearest phone box and got through to J.J. who didn't seem all that pleased to hear from me. 'I hope it's something important. I'm watching a film on television.' He cleared his throat. 'A rather good spy story.'

'I've had a busy evening,' I said. 'I found out that Yates made a call at a house in Middlesham.'

'What house?' J.J. said sharply.

'Three Gables,' I said. 'It belongs to an old friend of ours. Colin Avory. I paid a call on him myself.'

There was a long pause. 'Oh, yes,' J.J. said finally. 'How did you find him?'

'Dead,' I said. Deciding to keep the rest to myself, I hung up the phone before he could answer me. After that I went off for a meal, and eventually reached my flat about ten, just in time to pick up the ending of the spy film that J.J. had been watching on television. 'You've earned yourself a good rest,' the Chief of MI5 was saying to a tough looking agent who had just successfully wrapped up a mission. 'You'd better go off to the Caribbean for a holiday. Take a month.' I went off to bed chuckling at the thought that J.J.

It was all so vivid that I could hear my pursuer breathing heavily behind me like a man in pain.

might start handing out holidays in the sun to his agents. It was the only good laugh I had all that day.

I had a bad night with dreams full of death and fear. The worst one of them all was one in which I found myself in a pitch black country lane, running for my life towards two tiny lights glimmering in the far distance. I kept running, and all the time I could hear footsteps behind me, coming closer all the time. It was all so vivid that I could hear my pursuer breathing heavily behind me like a man in pain. Then he was on me and we were struggling in the darkness, with the lights coming nearer and nearer to us. His hands were at my throat and I couldn't breathe, but somehow I managed to bring up a fist, and he fell away from me in slow motion. Suddenly the lights were on top of me, two white glaring orbs that reminded me of the interrogation lights that had blazed down on me for hours, not so long ago when I had fallen for a brief while into the hands of the other side. It was then that I woke up screaming and found I was safe and sound in my own bed. I got up whistling cheerily, not the least bit disturbed by my nightmares. When you lead the sort of life I do, you have to expect that sort of dream.

There was a spatter of applause from the audience as the curtain fell for the last time. I groped for my raincoat and stared across the row of seats in front of me. I wasn't feeling very happy. I had sat through the whole show, staring at the aisle seat which would have been occupied by Colin Avory if someone hadn't put a bullet through him. I had sat and watched, with the brassy music banging away in my ears, hoping that someone would occupy the seat next to his. But no one had. I was therefore back where I had started, except for the knowledge that Avory had been mixed up in the whole dirty business. There was one faint hope left. I hurried down into the foyer, just in time to catch the ticket clerk before he put the shutter down.

'Excuse me,' I said. 'This seat number and the next one to it –' Even as I produced the ticket I had taken from Avory's wallet, I was wondering why I was wasting my time. The tickets had probably been bought by Avory, anyway, or in some ticket agency with cash. But there was no harm in trying.

I pushed the ticket under his nose.

'Somebody bought tickets for this seat and the seat next to it for other nights. That sort of thing doesn't happen very often. I'm wondering if by chance the reservations were made here – and if so by whom? Do you think. . . .'

My voice trailed away for the man behind the grill was glaring at me ill-temperedly.

'Is this a joke?' he demanded.

'Joke?'

'*You* bought the tickets.'

My heart missed a beat.

'I beg your pardon?'

He sniffed and cleared his throat irritably.

'As you yourself say, it isn't very often that someone comes in and reserves the same two seats for various nights – especially after the bad criticisms this show has received. I remember you distinctly, sir, and the grease stain on your left lapel. Good-night!' And pointedly he turned away and left me, silent and astounded.

I left the theatre, choosing to ignore the booking clerk's chilling insult regarding my tired old suit. *I had bought the tickets!* That's what he'd said.

'Impossible!' I muttered. 'The man's a fool.' And yet . . . and yet. . . .

There had been a ring of truth about his words. It was the sort of situation that you might find in one of those cinema thrillers which are always resolved at the end with a series of complicated but rational explanations. But this wasn't the cinema and that sort of thing doesn't happen in real life. Or so I thought until now.

But my shocks for the day were not yet over. Not by a long chalk.

I arrived back in my flat in a state bordering on panic. I fumbled for the switch, but I was now in such a state of nerves that I couldn't find it immediately. My hand slid frantically over the wall until my fingers fastened on it at last. It was at that precise moment – as the light came on – that I felt a tremendous pain at the back of my head. I had a quick vision of the familiar furniture, and then there was only the darkness again, and then nothing.

When I came to again it was to find myself lying stretched out on my bed. A thin, grey early morning light was coming into the room. I crawled to my feet and looked at my watch. Six o'clock. With my head throbbing I went into the living room and tried to figure it out. None of it seemed to make any sense. I could understand someone wanting to deal with me as they had dealt with Yates. What I couldn't understand was why they had attacked me, and then just left me there arranged tidily on the bed. Clearly the time had come for me to have a heart to heart talk with J.J.

As I was there long before nine, J.J. opened the door to me himself. He gave me a curious look. 'You look as if you've had another of your busy nights. Come in.'

I followed him into a living room of dark, heavy furniture. There was also a large mirror on the wall, which gave the room a curious elongated look.

'J.J.' I said, 'I'm sure you won't believe half of this.' Then I told him everything that had happened, right from the very beginning. 'You can understand how frightening the whole thing seems to me. Especially the ticket business.' I suddenly felt tired and defeated, and on the spur of the moment I decided to tell J.J. about the black-outs I had been having. He listened to this with the same quiet attention he had shown to my recital.

'These black-outs,' J.J. said. 'How long do they last?'

'Hours,' I said. 'A whole evening or day, sometimes.' Suddenly I realised something. 'Probably I wasn't attacked last night. Probably I just blacked out again.'

'I would think that was probable,' J.J. said drily. 'Especially as you were seen prowling around here last night.' He saw the expression on my face. 'Obviously you didn't know that. It's a strange business, isn't it? But we can talk about that later. The important thing is, I know who our double agent is, even if you don't.'

As if from a long way off I heard my voice, cracked and thin, saying: 'Would you like to tell me who he is?'

'I can do more than that,' J.J. said pleasantly. 'I can produce him for you. He's there. Right behind you.'

I swung around and found myself looking at my reflection, staring wild eyed at me from the mirror.

The Great Race for Dawson

The miner grinned at Dave and jerked a thumb over his shoulder.

'Good ground that, under the snow. There's gonna be a sizeable unclaimed area which'll be open to the first man to stake his claim on it and get it filed on the records at the new Records Office in Dawson.'

Dave Gilroy vowed that he was going to win that race. Big, black-bearded, black-toothed Bill Rogan, the camp bully, swore that he would be the winner. And Rogan would stop at nothing!

There was much excitement on the Yukon. The Canadian commissioners had come over the winter trail with an escort of Mounted Police for the official measuring of the gold claims.

When young Dave Gilroy, one of the many miners who had come north to the Klondike in the hopes of striking it rich, and found only heartbreak instead, heard of the measuring of the claims he had buttonholed a grisly-looking old miner, and asked him what it all meant.

'The measurin', sonny?' the old miner cackled. 'Why the measurin's as good as the first gold rush itself. You see, boy, when the first strike was made, every man was entitled ter stake out a length o' gold bearin' ground above an' below the original strike claim. Many o' the lads in thar enthusiasm took more than they was allowed, an' them thar commissioners is hyar ter put things right.'

Dave hurried to the fields where the measuring was already in progress. The commissioners were there all right, working in the sub-zero temperature

139

with instruments and tapes. They were being watched from all sides by fur-clad miners with hopeful expressions on their bearded faces.

'What's happening?' Dave asked an eager-looking, tobacco-chewing man who held a claim stake with his name crudely written on it.

The man jerked his thumb in the direction of the commissioners.

'They figger that claims 24 and 25 above the original is longer than it oughta be, boy. Good ground that, under the snow. Could make a man a millionaire. When they've finished measurin' there's gonna be a sizeable unclaimed area between the two which'll be open to the first man to stake his claim on it, and get it filed on the records at the new Records Office in Dawson.'

Dave glanced round. There were perhaps fifty fur-clad hopefuls standing by with claim sticks in their gloved hands, bare sledges waiting nearby with yapping dog teams in harness, ready to move off at the first crack of the whip.

Dave heard someone say in a low voice: 'Keep yore eye on thet thar commissioner. Every second's gonna count when he gives the word on thet new claim!'

That was enough for Dave.

It was a hard run back to his shack, and Dave was all thumbs as he harnessed up his team to the rusty old sledge that had brought him overland from St Michael on the coast six months ago. He was thankful now that he hadn't sold his shaggy coated team of dogs, as so many other disappointed miners had, when the going got tough. He always reckoned on going back the same way he'd come in, even if he went without an ounce of gold dust in his poke. Now the team was going to prove its worth in the long hustle north to Dawson.

Hurriedly he whittled out a claim stick, and wrote his name on it with a piece of charcoal, grabbed up a mallet from his little heap of personal belongings in the corner, and skidded out of the primitive shack on the hard snow.

As he mushed his team back to the site of the claim measuring he was hoping the findings hadn't been made known yet. Luck was patting his shoulder that day for as he drove up, the runners of his sledge screeching on the white blanket of snow, the crowd was where he had left them, and the commissioners were already busily comparing notes.

Black-bearded, black-hearted Bill Rogan, the camp bully, guffawed through his broken snags of teeth when Dave came galloping over to rejoin the crowd at the claims. Like Dave he too was holding his claim stick in his hand, just waiting for the word to go.

'Haw, haw! Yuh might as well give up now, Gilroy!' he bellowed hoarsely. 'You ain't got a chance against me, boy. Nobody has. I got me the best dog team in the Northlands. I'll be pushin' snow in your puny face all the way from hyar to Dawson!'

Whatever young Dave might have said in reply to the bully's taunts was lost as the chief commissioner looked up from his notebook, and announced to the eager assembly: 'Claims 24 and 25 are overmarked by a distance of twenty feet. Therefore this new area which I call Number 24A is hereby opened for claim!'

The miners surged forward in a solid, yelling mass.

A hundred nailed boots crashed over the rich, vacant area of gold bearing ground, and fifty hammers pounded like a blacksmith's forge gone crazy.

Dave had his stake in the iron-hard, frozen snow, and was hammering furiously with his mallet. It bore his name for all to see but, of course, nothing could be legalised until the claim had been filed in the new Records Office in Dawson, fifty miles to the north.

The entire claim was staked out with claim boards until a man could hardly walk without tripping over one.

Dave banged hard. The white snow was as solid as granite, and unless the stake was firmly driven in it was not deemed valid. Next to him Bully Bill Rogan hammered with all the strength in his powerful shoulders.

Rogan leered at young Dave: then he swung outwards with his hammer, and brought it down hard. Dave barely got his foot out of the way in time as the hammer blow descended. If that had caught him the race would have been over as far as he was concerned.

Duffy Bailey forgot to remove his hand from the top of his claim stick fast enough, and dealt himself a resounding blow to the knuckles which brought him howling to the snow, gripping the injured hand to his chest. No racing for him today. It needed two good hands to control a Northlands dog team and sledge.

Beaver Olsen swung up his hammer for the final blow to his stick, and off flew the head. As he knelt contemplating the headless handle, the head was descending from the blue on the other side of the claim.

It struck Digger Galvin plumb on top of the head, and bounced off to the ground. Digger slowly rose to his feet, surveying the busy assembly.

'All right, sports,' he howled in a hurt tone of voice, 'who's handin' out the rough stuff?'

Then his face was suffused by a smile as warm as the summer sun, as he sank to the snow to take no further interest in the proceedings.

Dave gave one last hard blow, threw his mallet to the snow, jumped to his feet, and began to run to his sledge over on the wintry trail. Bully Rogan and a dozen others were already in front of him. The black bearded bully was running beside his sledge, cracking his whip over the heads of his dogs as they strained into their harness.

Dave leaped on to the back of his sledge, gripped the back rail in one hand, and cracked his long whip in the icy air.

'Mush, mush!' he yelled as loudly as he could, and the sledge moved off through the snow on its greased runners.

All about him the other claimants were doing the same, the lone trail to the north was almost blocked by the number of dog-pulled sledges racing side by side.

The biting air was full of snow thrown up by the sledge runners in front of Dave, and he had to blink his eyes to clear them. Right now he was content to hold his yapping, tail-thumping team in, although others were in front of him on the trail. It was all of fifty miles, hard and exacting miles to Dawson on the north bank of the Klondike, and the weaker teams would be tiring long before the halfway mark.

As the greased runners of his sledge ate up the miles the pace was starting to tell on the weak as Dave knew it would. Although he made no move to increase his speed, content to allow his dogs to lope along in their own sweet time, he was overtaking sledge after sledge. Very soon he realised that those still in the great race for a fortune would be there at the finish, and it was time to force the pace a little.

The knotted end of his whip snaked out over the heads of the barking team leaders, and his cry of 'Mush, mush!' told them to lay forward into the harness, to run for all they were worth.

Beaver Olsen, ahead of Dave, turned his head to view what was behind, and saw Dave coming up on him inch by purposeful inch. He raised a clenched fist, and opened his mouth to yell an insult, forgetting that the fist he raised was holding the reins. Feeling the jerk the team leaders obeyed it, and swerved to the left as they figured that Beaver wanted them to do.

Sledge and team collided with that driven by that dour Scotsman, Angus McWhirter, and both men were hurled hard to the snow.

When Dave passed them the two men were squaring up to each other in good old-fashioned style, while their respective dog teams sat in the snow regarding each other with tail-thumping gestures of friendship.

The field was clearing. The sledges were strung out over ten miles of snow-laden trail, and Indian River was just round the bend.

An hour later Dave was up with the leaders. He could see that Bully Bill Rogan was leading the field, and that Dandy Clarence Smudgeley was holding hard to second place.

Whip in hand, monocle in eye, Dandy Clarence had met and overcome a variety of difficulties during his years as an officer of a highly regarded British cavalry regiment in India, but he was not prepared for the awful moment when a lone, gaunt timber wolf poked its snout through the winter brush on the ridge to the west, and howled an invitation to any and every canine with a friendly disposition within a radius of two miles.

A quick yap along the line of the team assured them that they were all of the same mind, and they went shooting off the trail towards the slope where the easy-going timber wolf was waiting.

Dandy Clarence was thrown off the sledge, and rolled in the powdery snow for a dozen feet before he realised what had happened. Then he scrambled to an upright position, fixed his gleaming monocle firmly in place, and went floundering off in the wake of his departing team of dogs.

'I say, what ho, you blighters!' he called clearly. 'Come back here, blast your mangy hides!'

Thus Dandy Clarence Smudgeley was out of the running.

Dave was grinning. The entire field, with the exception of Bully Bill Rogan was far behind him, and the way things were going he should reach Dawson far ahead of the black-bearded, black-toothed bully.

They crossed the ice on the Indian River almost neck and neck – and Bully Bill Rogan was furious.

Dave, inexperienced of such men as Rogan, could not help shouting a greeting:

'How about it now, Rogan? 24A or bust – and I reckon you're busted this time!'

It was more than Rogan could bear. To be beaten by an ignorant tenderfoot. Well, it wouldn't be that way, not as long as Bully Bill Rogan had a dirty trick or two up his flea-bitten sleeve.

Neck and neck they were climbing the snowy bank of the Indian on the north bank when Rogan suddenly jerked hard on his traces, bringing his yapping team hard round in a tight arc which cut right across Dave's path. To avoid a collision the youngster had no choice but to pull round in an even tighter circle, as Rogan guessed he would.

Dave felt the sledge tipping, and there was nothing he could do to stop it. He jumped clear of the falling steel mass, and ploughed a furrow in the snow with his nose in a very painful skid.

He lay there for a while, then raised his head, and shook it to clear the snow from his eyes. There was Rogan, head jerked round to view the discomfiture of his rival, and laughing like a drain in full flood.

'Who's busted now, Gilroy?' was his parting remark, and he had disappeared over the rise in the ground.

'Of all the dirty, low-down – just wait until I get my hands on him!' roared Dave as he pulled himself out of the snow, and surveyed the chaos of his sledge and team.

The team leader, Whipper, was surveying his master with a melancholy air, and Dave felt himself bound to pat the disreputable looking hound on the head before he burst into tears.

'It wasn't your fault, Whipper,' he told the shaggy dog. 'It was that other cur, Rogan!'

And then Dave felt obliged to apologise for putting Whipper in the same miserable class as the black-toothed villain.

It took him half-an-hour to right his sledge, and untangle the mess of harness and reins that the upset had caused. The short winter day was drawing to a close, but he knew he had to continue through the darkness because that was what Bully Rogan would be doing.

As long as it was dark the going was slow. It would have been dangerous to do otherwise. From time to time Dave hauled his panting, tongue-lolling team to a halt to give them a rest, and also to listen for any sounds other than the chill howl of the wind coming out of the north.

Towards dawn he was sure he could hear the hiss of sledge runners not far ahead, and guessed that Rogan was just in front of him. Both men had crossed the ice-bound Klondike during the small hours, and were now travelling due west towards Dawson.

When the sun rose in a kind of murky orange haze over the mountains of the northeast, Dave forced his heavy eyelids apart, and suddenly gave vent to an exuberant whoop of joy.

Bully Rogan was not more than two hundred yards in front of him, the burly bearded villain of the gold camp shambling along in a bear-like run beside his sledge, and exhorting his dogs with vicious slashes of his whip.

Dave followed the bully's example. He could afford to now, and foot by foot he decreased the distance between them.

When he heard the snapping and yapping of the team behind him, Rogan turned his head, and the expression of utter disbelief on his ugly face was almost ludicrous.

Dave was close enough to shout to his rival: 'Dawson's just over the ridge, Rogan. I reckon 24A's going to be mine!'

'The devil it is!' snarled Rogan in reply, and to Dave's astonishment the bully reached down into the heap of furs on his sledge, and when he came upright he was holding a rifle in his hand!

The muzzle swung to cover Dave, and Rogan's face was set in an animal snarl as his finger tightened on the trigger.

Dave hurled himself flat to the snow as flame spurted from the end of the barrel, and he gave a cry of pain as the hot breath of the bullet seared his shoulder.

He buried his face in the snow, playing possum until Rogan was ahead again. The bullet had merely grazed him in passing, but if Rogan believed him to be still alive he would not hesitate to come back and finish the job.

The dog team came to a halt on the hard packed snow, and shaggy Whipper whimpered as he led his fellow canines back to where Dave lay without moving. Dave felt the warm, roughness of the husky's tongue as it licked his cheek. He opened his eyes, and said soothingly: 'It's all right, Whipper. We'll be on our way in a minute.'

With Dawson in sight Dave knew Rogan wouldn't dare to shoot again, and as the wooden buildings of the town on the Klondike came into sight he was again right on Rogan's heels.

Old Jimmy was a panhandler. He lived in a shack on the outskirts of town, and did odd jobs around the saloons and dance-halls of Dawson. He was a nice old man, everybody liked him, and so he liked them in return.

But Old Jimmy had a long memory for those who had done him wrong in the past, and he remembered Bully Bill Rogan from the days when the hulking brute had come up the Yukon from St Michael a year ago. He had felt the weight of Rogan's heavy fist on that occasion, and if the bully had forgotten all about it, Jimmy hadn't.

That very same fur-clad bully was now puffing down the main street beside his sledge with Dave in hot pursuit, and Old Jimmy was the first human being Rogan saw. He gripped the front of the old man's ragged buffalo coat in his thick fingers, thrust his black-toothed face in front of him, and snarled:

'Hey, yuh old wreck. Where's the new Records Office?'

'Take yore paws off me!' yapped Old Jimmy angrily, and the next moment was sent reeling by a vicious blow from the bully's fist. As he measured his length on the snow Rogan clamped his boot down on the old-timer's chest.

'The Records Office?' he snarled. 'Where is it?'

Old Jimmy pointed a trembling finger towards the saloon down the street where half-a-dozen men were lined up in an orderly queue by the door.

Rogan snarled in his beard, and ran hard, panting every inch of the way. The six men standing with their hands thrust deep in their pockets, and looks of intense gloom on their faces, glanced at Rogan as he slithered to a halt beside them.

'My name's Rogan!' he bawled at them. 'I'm going in there first. Anybody got any objections?'

They all shook their heads rapidly. They didn't mind in the least. Rogan thrust the door open and nearly bowled over the mild-mannered man just inside.

'I'm first!' snarled Rogan, displaying his blackened and broken teeth. 'Yew wanna argue?'

'Not at all, sir,' smiled the mild man. 'Yes sir, I can certainly see why you wanted to jump the queue. Come right inside.'

Old Jimmy was rising to his feet as Dave Gilroy halted his sledge in front of him. He had seen what happened, and now he helped the oldster to his feet.

'Are yew a friend of his?' Old Jimmy wanted to know.

Dave grinned and shook his head. 'Definitely not. We were racing to file a claim on the river. Looks like after all my trouble, I've lost.'

'Lost?' Old Jimmy howled with laughter, and slapped his bony knee in enjoyment. 'Lost? Yew ain't lost, son.' He pointed his arm in a different direction to that which he had indicated to Rogan. 'That's the Records Office over thar, boy. Yew get in thar, and file thet claim o' yourn!'

'But what about Rogan?' Dave wanted to know. 'What's that place with the queue outside?'

But Old Jimmy was still laughing uproariously at his private joke, so Dave left him to it.

He was still laughing when Dave came triumphantly out of the office with 24A securely registered in his name. No one could take it from him now, not even Bully Rogan.

As he stood in the pale, wintry sunshine with his dogs, patting them on their heads, and promising them a new life of luxury, the saloon door suddenly swung wide open – and Bully Rogan came staggering out into the daylight. His hands were pressed to his mouth, and as he passed Dave in the snow he gave him a vicious, but painful snarl. It was then that Dave realised why Old Jimmy was laughing. For where there had been a double row of black teeth in Rogan's mouth, now there was – nothing!

Dave shouted to Old Jimmy across the street.

'Hey, what was that place you sent Rogan to?'

'Hee, hee, it war a travelling dentist,' the old-timer told him gleefully. 'Arrived yesterday and set up shop in the saloon. Took six of the tooth-jerker's pals to hold Bully Rogan down while the dentist pulled his teeth! Hee hee!'

Bully Rogan, the man who had raced for a fortune but found instead an obliging dentist in dire need of money, was now a figure of fun from St Michael to Skagway. There was nothing to do but pull out for a different climate, and hope to outrun the story.

As for Dave, he settled down to work his claim, and was one of the few miners to come out of the Klondike with a fortune. But as long as he lived he never forgot the great race for 24A, and Old Jimmy's helping hand.

Undersea Patrol

Hector Timberlake was an interfering politician who was out to see that the Undersea Patrol was disbanded. 'A waste of public money,' he called it.

Then Timberlake was kidnapped by a gang of slick pirates. It seemed poetic justice that only the Undersea Patrol could rescue the man who was dedicated to wiping it out of existence.

The Patrol Commander's face was as bleak and craggy as a granite cliff, his voice as chill as an arctic wind: 'In view of the circumstances, lieutenant, I have no choice but to reprimand you. You have admitted using official equipment – our underwater radio – to contact your brother aboard another ship for purely personal reasons.'

Standing stiffly at attention on the other side of the desk in the Commander's office in Patrol HQ, Lieutenant Ray Winter thought grimly: 'And all because of that interfering old busybody, Timberlake!'

'So consider yourself reprimanded. It will be noted on your official file . . .' The Commander's face softened into a smile. 'But don't think I wouldn't have done the same. Timberlake's a politician, out to get the Patrol, and he'll use any means to hand. This time he happens to be using you. Now let's move on to something more interesting . . . how did *Seacub's* test cruise go?'

Young Ray relaxed. Enthusiasm entered his voice. 'Fine, sir, she's better than anything else we've got. Really ideal for underwater rescue work.'

The Commander nodded. 'But expensive. Getting the whole Patrol equipped with *Seacub* will cost a fortune. And Timberlake's gunning for us, keeps on about taxes and how the Patrol is a waste of public money – '

'That's rubbish,' Ray said hotly.

'You don't have to convince me, lieutenant. Would you say *Seacub* is ready to go into service?'

'Yes sir, she's passed every test in the book, and some that aren't. She's just rarin' to go.'

'Right,' the Commander said briskly. 'You'll take her out on routine patrol at dawn tomorrow. Dismiss . . . and good luck.'

'Aye, aye, sir!'

Ray Winter threw up a salute and wheeled from the office. Outside, he tossed his cap in the air, fielded it and rushed to his cabin with the news.

His Australian crewmate, 'Blue' Shaw, switched off the TV news announcer who was just saying: '. . . today, Thursday the twelfth, January 2001.'

'Well, how'd it go, sport? Keel-hauling, or forty days in the brig?'

'A rep – and we're sailing *Seacub* tomorrow.'

'Yair, another dawn patrol.' Blue shed his sea-green uniform and turned down the sheets on his bunk. 'Me for some shut-eye, cobber.'

After breakfast, Ray and Blue walked briskly down to the dock where *Seacub* was berthed. Blue was not at his best in the early morning. 'Friday the thirteenth,' he groused. 'What'll you bet something goes wrong?'

Looking at *Seacub,* Ray found it hard to imagine anything going wrong. The submarine was shiny new, a fat oval shape; most of her inside space was empty – to be filled with survivors if they had to make a rescue.

They sailed out into the Atlantic. The grey surface was empty of shipping, for now all shipping, luxury liner and commercial transport alike, travelled beneath the surface. And there was plenty of traffic: fast sleek subs, safe from the weather menace up top, carrying imports and exports.

Ray began to think about his brother, Mike, who was a crew-man aboard the luxury liner, *Triton.* 'And now I can't even have a chat with him on the radio,' he muttered. 'That Timberlake's a perishing menace.'

Seacub performed perfectly and Ray and Blue settled down to routine. Then, halfway across the Atlantic, the underwater radio crackled to life . . .

'*Mayday . . . Mayday! US Triton calling. We have engine failure. Mayday –*'

Abruptly the distress signal cut off.

'Get her bearings,' Ray yelled.

Blue, at the sonar screen, nodded grimly as he moved the dials. 'I knew it,

Friday the thirteenth . . .' Then, 'I've got her!' He sang out range and bearing.

Ray aimed *Seacub* like an arrow and homed in at top speed. Modern submarines were near accident-proof, but when they were in trouble it was bad trouble. The worst. Undersea, with an enormous pressure of water waiting outside to crush the hull and crew to pulp.

Ray's heart beat faster as he thought of Mike aboard the *Triton* . . .

Seacub raced through the deep on her errand of mercy and he worried: was *Triton* already a mangled hulk? What could have gone wrong?

Blue, watching the sonar screen, said: 'Another sub just leaving *Triton!*'

They were close enough now to use the searchlight and Ray switched it on. As the powerful beam cut through the blue-green sea it lit up a submarine carrying the letters UP on her side. Undersea Patrol.

'I don't recognise her,' Blue said.

Ray flashed her on the radio – and got no answer. As he closed in on *Triton,* the mystery sub disappeared. Puzzled, Ray manoeuvred in close to the luxury ship, cutting speed to match her drift.

Then the unique feature of the rescue sub came into play. Powerful electro-magnets clamped the two ships together, a cylindrical air-lock fitting over the escape hatch.

As he flooded the connecting chamber with air and opened the inner seal, Ray prayed that Mike was still alive . . .

He went through quickly, opened *Triton's* escape hatch and – walked right into a rough-house. A massive fist clouted him between the eyes, staggering him. Strong hands gripped him and pulled him down. Someone shouted: 'Got the blighter!'

Ray struggled futilely under a welter of bodies and fists. The breath gasped out of his lungs as his head slammed against a metal deck. He heard, faintly, a familiar voice:

'Stop! That's my brother – this really is the Patrol this time!'

Minutes later, still groggy but standing unaided and sipping a tot of rum, he listened to Mike explain: 'We thought the kidnappers had come back, only this time we were ready for 'em.'

'Kidnappers?' Ray echoed, frowning. 'What's going on down here?'

'It was Bull Kramer's gang. He had a man planted in our crew, sabotaged the engine and radio and we didn't suspect a thing. Along comes a sub labelled UP – a bit quick, but we're glad to see her. Then there are guns covering us and they grab the richest passenger aboard to hold for ransom. A man called Hector Timberlake – '

'Timberlake!' Ray thought grimly of poetic justice. Timberlake had called the Patrol useless. Maybe he was changing his mind now . . .

Triton's captain announced: 'The damage is not serious – we'll be under way in an hour.'

'And I'll go after Kramer,' Ray said. He squeezed Mike's arm. 'Be seeing you.'

Back on *Seacub,* he told Blue what was going on. 'The nerve of it, pretending to be a Patrol ship – if we don't get Timberlake back before he has to pay ransom, our name'll be mud and the Patrol finished.'

Ray pushed the rescue sub into a wide arc with the sonar scanning at maximum range.

'Sub on screen,' Blue said, and called range and bearing.

'Must be Kramer,' Ray said, changing course to follow the kidnap sub, driving ahead at top speed.

The two ships ploughed through the inky depths, pursued and pursuer, with *Seacub* gradually gaining. High speed was one of the essential features of the rescue sub.

'We're going to catch 'em,' Blue growled with satisfaction. 'Coming up on 'em fast.'

Then –

'Heck, she's surfacing!'

Ray angled his ship upward through the water, following the blip on the sonar screen. He broke surface and saw a blue-grey sky above the Atlantic, a sea almost as smooth as a sheet of glass – and Kramer's sub, surfaced, heading for a rendezvous with a seaplane!

The plane was already floating on the water.

'They're going to fly Timberlake off – if they succeed, we'll never catch 'em!'

Recklessly, Ray aimed *Seacub* between the other submarine and the seaplane, charging headlong at high speed, building up a wash.

Someone shouted: 'Watch it – Patrol ship!'

As Ray came in on collision course, Kramer swerved away. Ray veered towards the seaplane. The pilot, alarmed, began to taxi across the water, with Ray in pursuit . . . seeing the Patrol sub still following, he gunned his engines and took off, circling overhead.

'Stopped that little game,' Ray muttered. 'Now just how do we go about getting Timberlake back?'

But Kramer wasn't waiting. As the seaplane took to the air, he shouted: 'Crash dive!'

The kidnap sub sank beneath the surface and Ray had no choice but to follow her down. 'Try the radio, Blue – there might be another Patrol sub in range.' But he doubted it. Underwater radio was still a short-range affair.

Blue spun dials and sent their call signal. 'No dice,' he reported.

Deeper into the ocean they sank, Blue watching the sonar screen as they closed in on Kramer. Suddenly he yelled: 'They're turning back on us. Maybe she's trying to ram!'

Ray doubted it, but changed course.

'Ray!' Blue's voice sounded shaken as he watched a blip on the screen. 'Torpedo . . . they're trying to torpedo us!'

Desperately Ray swung the wheel, calling for full power from the engines. He held his breath, waiting for the explosion, knowing they had no chance if the torpedo struck.

Blue's hands clenched. 'Killers! They'll stop at nothing!'

But the deadly torpedo passed them, by a hair's breadth. Watching the track on sonar, Ray and Blue sighed with relief . . . until they noticed that Kramer had taken advantage of the diversion to dive deep.

He was still going down, boring into the inky depths at high speed away from *Seacub*.

Ray went down after him, with Blue glued to the sonar in case Kramer tried another torpedo. As they sank lower, there was a sudden change in the underwater current. They hit a layer of warm water – and the reaction between cold and warm layers made their sonar go haywire.

Ray went deeper hoping to get clear of the interference, praying he would not lose Kramer. Anxious minutes passed before Blue reported:

'I'm getting a clear reading again. But he's far ahead now.'

Ray pushed *Seacub* on to the new course and the chase continued . . . gradually, they caught up again. Then, without warning, the Patrol sub bucked and rocked violently, like a leaf blown about in a gale.

Blue, clinging to the handrail, gasped: 'What's going on now?' *Seacub* continued to shudder. The sonar screen showed an incredible sight.

Ray said grimly: 'I've only seen this once before – it's an undersea volcano erupting!'

He put *Seacub* through a tight arc, racing away from the scene of the eruption. Outside the hull, the sea boiled in elemental fury as molten lava exploded upwards from the sea-bed, hurling out great chunks of rock from the volcanic crater.

The sonar was blotted out now; there was no chance of tracking anything in the maelstrom of boiling water.

The sea boiled in elemental fury as molten lava exploded upwards from the sea-bed, hurling out great chunks of rock from the volcanic crater.

'So Kramer will get clear away,' Blue said bitterly.

'I only hope *we* do!'

Ray kept on full power till he was clear. The eruption died away and the sonar screen cleared. Ray circled again, hunting.

For minutes nothing happened and they were beginning to feel despair when the radio pulsed with an urgent voice:

'*Mayday, mayday! Kramer calling* – '

'Kramer!' Blue gasped. 'Some trick, I bet.'

Ray gestured for silence as Kramer's voice continued: 'We're trapped on the sea-bed. Part of the hull smashed in the eruption. We're pinned under a rockfall. We can't last long . . . Help us . . . Help . . .'

'It could be a trap,' Blue said doubtfully.

But Ray shook his head. 'We've got to take the risk – this may be our only chance to grab Timberlake back.'

While Blue plotted range and bearing on the radio signal Ray set the course. They were going back, no matter what the risk. Cautiously, he edged *Seacub* back into the volcanic area – but the crater was sleeping again.

Searchlight on, Ray peered through the fore porthole; the sea-bed was littered with rubble, great rocks and now-solid lava. They passed over chasms where volcanic gas still escaped.

Then he saw Kramer's sub, or part of it. It lay on its side, half-buried beneath a mountain-sized slab of rock. The kidnappers were fairly trapped.

Ray circled warily, studying the damage. The aft part of the ship appeared unharmed and watertight; and there was life aboard. Their radio kept appealing for help . . .

Blue said uneasily: 'This ain't healthy, skipper – that volcano could blow up again without warning.'

Ray nodded, then blanked off his mind to the danger. There was nothing he could do about that. His job was to rescue the men trapped in the submarine.

One thing was certain: the sub couldn't move. That meant he had to take the crew off. He closed in slowly, matching his airlock to their escape hatch. Sweat ran down his face as he manœuvred, aware of the towering rock overhead . . .

Finally, he was ready for exchange.

'Listen, Kramer,' he said over the radio. 'This is the Patrol. We're ready to take you off, so listen well. Timberlake comes first. Then members of your crew, one by one, and unarmed. Yourself last. Is that clear?'

'Clear,' Kramer answered. 'You've got to move fast. One bulkhead's already strained to the limit. It could go at any moment.'

Ray, with a hefty spanner in one hand, stood to one side of the inner hatch as he opened it. He had not long to wait. The opposite hatch opened and a big figure came through the chamber, fast, gun in hand. Kramer.

Ray smiled coldly. He had been expecting a double-cross and was ready. He swung the spanner. But he had not been expecting the speed and power of Bull Kramer. The kidnapper swerved, and the spanner caught him only a glancing blow.

The gun in his hand swung up to point at Ray. Ray dived low. The gun exploded, scorching Ray's face. The bullet went past his head and buried itself harmlessly in a store locker.

Ray got both hands on Kramer's wrist and twisted. The gun slithered across the steel deck.

Blue scooped it up. 'Stand back, Ray – I've got him covered!'

Ray hardly heard his crewmate. Kramer's big fists were slamming into him like sledge-hammers and he was hitting back as hard as he could. Locked together, they wrestled on the deck, rolling over and over, till Ray got in one telling blow to the heart. It carried all his weight and fury, and Kramer went white and collapsed.

Breathing hard, Ray stood up. 'Lock him away,' he grunted, and Blue dragged the unconscious gang boss aft.

Ray spoke into the radio. 'It didn't work, and Kramer's under lock and key. If Timberlake doesn't come through next, I'll abandon the rest of you.'

The threat worked. Without their leader, the kidnappers went to pieces.

And so Hector Timberlake was the next to step through the escape hatch. For a fire-eating politician, he was smaller than Ray had imagined; and just now he looked rather battered. He looked even unhappier facing the gun in Ray's hand.

He gulped, and said: 'Er, I'm very pleased you got here, lieutenant.'

One by one, Kramer's crew came through; and one by one, Blue locked them away.

'Now, out of it, fast,' Ray snapped.

He was just in time, for as Blue disconnected the escape chamber, the huge rock over the trapped submarine began to topple. Slowly, but surely it came down, crushing the hull of Kramer's ship.

Ray turned the *Seacub* to head up and out . . . just as the volcano erupted again. For minutes it was touch and go as the sea boiled around them.

Timberlake, watching the sonar screen, looked quite sick as *Seacub* rocked violently. Then they were safe, and heading for home.

Hector Timberlake cleared his throat as the trip settled back into routine. 'I'd like to thank you men,' he said. 'It seems I was wrong about the Patrol.' His voice lifted, gaining power. 'But in future you'll have my full backing. I'll see the Patrol gets all the money it needs for new ships. And I'll be giving my commendation of you two heroes in person to your Commander the moment I step ashore!'

Ray winked at Blue, and gave the thumbs-up sign. Friday the thirteenth had turned out fine!

Ransom for a Colt

From his grandfather, Dan Burling had heard the story of Tom Cranbrook, the young highwayman, who mortally wounded had spoken of a hidden treasure. But no trace of the highwayman's plunder had ever been found.

It's whereabouts were to be revealed in the course of a hunt for yet another highwayman, Dan's erstwhile friend Jack Martindale.

Dan Burling rode the black colt round and round the paddock, now urging it on, now holding it in, occasionally halting it, and reining it back a few paces before letting it canter forward again, always demanding instant response. The colt was perfect in every way and Dan's young heart rejoiced at its perfection – rejoiced, too, that its breaking and schooling had been all his own work.

His father, now crippled from a riding accident a year before in 1773, sat in a chair by the gate and watched his son, occasionally shouting a word of warning or advice. Old Burling had broken and trained hundreds of colts in his time but now, unable to ride any more, he was happy to see that Dan was able to carry on under his instructions.

'I think we must call him Black Prince,' Dan shouted, as he took the colt past at an extended trot. 'He has manners fit for the king's court.'

From his seat on the gate Jack Martindale called out, 'Pity he's not a mare, he could be Black Bess and go to a highwayman, he's perfect for that – don't you think so, Dan?'

Dan glanced over to where young Jack Martindale, handsome and debonair, was idling the day away as usual, a straw in his mouth and his three-cornered hat tipped back on his head.

'The colt's perfect, right enough,' he replied, 'but I wouldn't let him go to a highwayman, not for all the gold in the Mint.'

In Jack's eyes highwaymen were the great heroes of the day – gentlemen of the road – taunting the forces of misrule and snapping their fingers at the gallows. They had created a tradition of reckless courage that had captured the imagination of the English at that time.

Not so Dan. It was a story told by his grandfather when Dan was a lad that had shown Dan the other, ugly side of a highwayman's life – the story of a wounded man and of a treasure hunt that never began.

Recollecting back into the distant days of his own youth, the old man told Dan of his friend Tom Cranbrook, who became a highwayman, and of a message brought by a passing postillion – 'Be you Samuel Burling, lad? Then 'tis from young Tom Cranbrook. He says to tell you he lies, nigh cut in half, at Newbury. He says for you to go to him quick like!'

Hurrying to Newbury, Dan's grandfather, then only eighteen, reached his friend's bedside just before he died – in time for a few whispered words. . . . 'The money, Sam – all yours now – down the tunnel in Hope Pit – in the lap of the god. Get it, it's for you!' Within the hour he was dead.

That story brought to an end Dan's youthful hero-worship of highwaymen. 'Now, Dan boy,' his grandfather had said, 'I shan't find the treasure now. If you can find out where Hope Pit is, you look in the lap of the god down the tunnel; if the money's still there it's yours to keep. Please God it'll bring you more happiness than it did young Tom Cranbrook.'

For a year or more, Dan had enquired of everyone he met whether they knew where Hope Pit might be, but no one knew of the place, and it was only Jack Martindale's mention of highwaymen that now brought the story of Tom Cranbrook back to his mind.

Dan rode the colt through into the yard where his father was leaning on his crutches ready to cast an expert eye as Dan bedded the horses down for the night. 'If only we could keep Black Prince,' Dan said, 'I'd love to have him for my own riding – just this one.'

'Nay, lad,' the old man replied sadly, 'such horses are not for the likes of us, specially with me being on crutches now and no money coming in. Nay, the colt must go to some gentleman's stables; he'll fetch twenty guineas, maybe more. You've done a good job on him, Dan lad.' Praise, this indeed, from an expert: but Dan yearned to keep the colt.

That night Dan woke suddenly with a feeling that something was wrong.

Slipping into his breeches he went to the back door, picking up his father's flint-lock gun as he went. He unbarred the door and looked out. Everything in the yard looked perfectly normal in the moonlight. Returning to the kitchen he took a piece of smouldering wood from the hearth and with it lit the candle in a lantern, and crossed to the stable. At first glance everything seemed normal there, until he came to Black Prince's stall. The colt's flanks gleamed in the feeble light of the lantern and steam rose from his back and neck. Who could have dared to take him out in the dead of night and ride him all to a sweat like this!

As Dan looked closer at the colt a shadowy figure slipped out from behind the door and fled into the night; and as it disappeared Dan thought he saw a small black object fall into the straw that was strewn behind the door. He called out, but whoever the intruder was he had disappeared. Who could this be, lurking in the stable at that hour? And how did it link up with the state that Black Prince was in? But Dan busied himself at once in rubbing the colt down, and did not leave until he was certain the horse was perfectly dry and rugged up.

This done he made a tour of inspection. The other horses were all in order – the old grey mare, the carthorse and the rest – nothing was out of place or missing. Then Dan's eye was caught by the black object lying in the straw by the door. Bending down he picked up a small black mask. Suddenly Dan remembered Jack's words about Black Prince being fit for a highwayman. Had Jack borrowed the colt to ride out as a highwayman, and Dan's arrival disturbed him just as he was returning his borrowed mount to the stable? Dan had no way of knowing for certain, but he aimed to find out.

Back in his bed once more, Dan turned the problem over and over in his mind. At last he hit upon a plan. Even the element of risk to himself that it involved was strangely to his liking. It required the help of old Ben, the cowman, but Dan knew he could rely on him.

First old Ben had his part to play, in the Plough Inn the following evening. Waiting until young Jack Martindale was well within earshot he announced to the company in general, 'I hear there be great goin's on over at Grange Hall tomorrow night!'

Sure enough some asked, 'What goin's on be they, Ben?'

'Why, haven't you heard? Sir John's cousin's comin' home – him what went to India and made his fortune there. Now he's so rich I reckon Sir John'll give him a real good welcome. He's staying at Blandford tonight and gets to the Grange tomorrow by nightfall.'

Old Ben noticed that Jack Martindale had been very attentive to all this.

Who could have dared to take out the colt in the dead of night and ride him all to a sweat like this?

Now it was Dan's turn.

He had already arranged to take their old coach to the wheelwright in a neighbouring town to have it repaired – a job that had been talked of for some time – and duly set off that morning. A day in stables would do Black Prince good.

But Dan never reached his destination. Instead he turned down a lane leading across country to the road Sir John's cousin from India would presumably be taking on his journey to Grange Hall. There he drove the coach into a small wood and waited for evening.

This waiting was the worst part, for it gave Dan time to think. Would his plan work? Would the highwayman, who ever he was, rise to the bait? Would he be there and, young fool that he was, risk the gallows for murder when challenged? Come what may Dan was determined to go through with his plan.

As the sun dropped out of sight Dan took the reins and drove the coach into the road leading to Grange Hall. The horses jogged on across the valley, then toiled up a steep hill, and they were on the edge of the heathland, an uncultivated, scrub-covered area, just such a place that a highwayman would choose for lying in wait.

Here Dan stopped and from the inside of the coach dragged a bulky object, remarkably like the top half of a man. It was draped in an old cloak of his father's and on its apex was a wide-brimmed hat. With two straps, cunningly placed, he fastened the whole straw-filled contraption on to the driver's seat, and stood back to examine the effect. Yes, in the dim light, it looked surprisingly lifelike. Then, perching himself on the pole between the two horses, Dan drove on from there. It was uncomfortable, but he managed well enough.

The horses jogged on along the rutted road, two miles further on to the heath. Still the highwayman had not shown up. Was his plan failing? Dan wondered.

Then a horseman moved into the road. Yes, there was no mistaking Black Prince, even in the twilight. Dan's heart beat faster as he crouched low between the horses as they jogged steadily on.

Moonlight gleamed on the barrel of a pistol, and a familiar voice rang out: 'Stand and deliver!' Jack Martindale yelled again at the top of his voice. Still the horses jogged on.

As they drew abreast of Jack, Dan heard him mutter 'Deaf as a post, by thunder!' Then louder and furiously, 'Pull up, you old fool. Do you want me to fill your belly with shot?'

When even this brought no response, Jack rode alongside the coach, cursing and swearing, and firing at point blank range at the stolid, straw-filled coachman, the only result being that the horses quickened their pace.

Dan slipped from the pole and crouched low on the road while the rumbling coach passed over 'him. Then he rose to his feet. 'All right, Jack, you're not a murderer yet,' he said, as Black Prince spun round and the pistol was aimed at his own head. 'Shoot me if you want to, Jack,' he continued, 'but you'll swing for it. Those horses are on their way home, and when they get there it's you the Redcoats will be looking for.'

All the swagger suddenly left Jack. He aimed his second pistol in a half-hearted way as Dan approached, but he did not pull the trigger, and he made no resistance when Dan wrenched it out of his hand.

'Now dismount!' Dan ordered. Jack obeyed without a word and Dan swung himself into the saddle. 'And if I see your stupid face in our village again, I'll tell of this night's work, you can be sure,' Dan warned as he cantered off to overtake the coach, leaving Jack standing speechless and foolish in the empty road.

After fitting a strong new lock on the stable door, Dan lay in bed that night feeling confident that Jack Martindale would leave and never trouble them again. Weary, but happy, he slept soundly.

He slept so soundly that he did not hear stealthy footsteps in the yard, the sound of cautiously splintered woodwork, of a horse's hooves as it was led quietly away.

In the morning the stable door was swinging with a broken lock, and Black Prince's stall was empty. Sure enough, Jack Martindale had left, but not without troubling them again. He had taken Black Prince with him and might already be many miles away.

Dan snatched a bite of breakfast, and hastily packing a saddle-bag he mounted the old grey mare and was away. He could only guess at the route Jack had probably taken, but a light sprinkle of snow had fallen during the night and soon his guess was confirmed; the track of a lone horseman showed clearly as it left the valley and struck off northwards across country. All morning the grey mare put the miles behind her. She was old, but fit and strong. The hoof-prints ahead were clear and Dan rode fast.

At noon they reached a highroad where the tracks were at once lost among those of many horsemen and wagons that had passed that way. Had Jack turned left or right? Dan was now in country that was strange to him, and he had no idea where the road led in either direction. On impulse he turned right. After following the road about half a mile he met a wagoner and stopped to ask whether the man had passed a young toff riding a black horse.

'Yes, that I have,' replied the wagoner, 'and a real beauty that young horse is, to be sure.' Then he added, 'He passed me just back along by Hope Pit.'

'Hope Pit!' Dan echoed, picturing a wounded highwayman and an unclaimed treasure of fifty years ago. As he rode on he noted the position of a large, disused chalk pit on his left, but Black Prince was the pressing business. The highwayman's treasure had waited fifty years, another few hours would not matter.

A steep hill ahead led down into a busy town. Dan did not know its name, but that did not matter. In the hubbub of the market square, the smell of food wafted from the door of a large inn, and told him how hungry he was. After all, was not the inn the very best place to gain news of a strange horseman passing that way? He handed the mare over to an ostler, waited long enough to see that the man knew his business, then made for the loud hum of conversation coming from the inn parlour.

The place was packed, for it was market day, and voices were loud, but there was one, youthful and cock-sure, that rose above the rest – 'I gave the old fool a shove and he was in the ditch, so I took his purse which was full –.' That voice was unmistakable, and Dan pushed through the throng to find Jack Martindale seated on a table, entertaining a circle of idlers and n'er-do-wells like himself.

Jack's hand went to his pistol, and the close circle suddenly widened and the hum of talk died away.

'If I'm to hang as a horse-thief,' Jack muttered through his teeth, 'I'll make it murder for good measure!' and he tried to level his pistol at Dan's head; but Dan acted quickly. Leaping forward he gave the table on which Jack was seated a mighty kick. The pistol shot drove harmlessly into a rafter above, and Jack and table together crashed backwards on to the sanded floor.

Dan picked up the pistol. 'You won't hang this time for anything,' he said, 'but I'll take the pistol in case you feel like shooting someone else!'

That was the last time Dan ever saw Jack Martindale.

Later that afternoon, well fed and rested, Dan rode Black Prince up to Hope Pit, leading the mare beside him. He tethered the horses and climbed the nettle-grown debris that half filled the pit, which had clearly not been worked for many years. Its floor was a tangled jungle of small trees and weeds which grew criss-crossed everywhere.

Dan searched the place for an hour or more without finding any trace of what he was looking for. Then, when he was almost convinced that there was no such thing as a tunnel there, he noticed a track leading in under the bole of a fallen elder tree – a track clearly made by foxes or badgers passing in and out over the years. But how was he to get under the tree? He tried lifting it, but it was half buried in fallen chalk and would not budge. He scraped the loose surface chalk away with his hands, but underneath it was packed hard and would need a pick to move it. Then, as a last resort, he pressed his back against the vertical side of the pit, and pushed the fallen tree with his heels. It shifted a couple of inches.

Readjusting his position, Dan strained his back and legs with all his might; this time the tree moved a foot or more. Another shift and another heave, and the whole mass collapsed. Tree, chalk and Dan together slid down the slope, and he found himself sprawling in what was clearly the opening of a badger's den.

Picking himself up, he peered into the hole; it seemed to get larger as it went back. He removed some loose chalk with his hands, then turned round and kicked some more back into the hole. Thus enlarged it was big enough for him to crawl into; but it would be pitch dark inside – he needed a light.

Remembering that he had included a small lantern when he packed the saddle-bag that morning, he returned to the horses. With flint and steel he lit the candle, and, thus equipped, returned to the hole. Lying flat on his stomach he then wormed his way through the entrance, pushing the lantern carefully ahead of him. Out in the daylight its light had seemed feeble, but here in the darkness it shone brightly. Sure enough, Dan saw to his delight that the tunnel grew much larger as it penetrated deeper into the chalk.

Once inside he got to his feet and found that he could walk, not upright, but crouching somewhat. His elbows brushed the walls on either side, walls which were polished smooth as though by the brushing of hundreds of elbows: the smooth floor under-foot suggested it had been trodden by hundreds of bare feet. The lantern light probed a few feet ahead as Dan moved forward, but beyond that all was darkness and mystery.

Dan moved steadily on, resisting the temptation to explore several side galleries that led off to right and left. When he had walked, as he judged, two hundred yards he saw the end of the passage approaching – not the dead end of a blank wall, but an opening into a larger space beyond. Full of expectation he approached to find himself in a domed cave, perfectly circular, perhaps ten paces across; but what held his attention immediately was an object in the centre of the floor. On a square base the crude image of a grotesque human figure sat, cross-legged. It was obviously carved in the solid chalk itself, but was stained dark as though by some dark liquid poured over it. Could it be blood? Dan imagined some barbaric human sacrifice being performed here in dim, prehistoric times.

What was it his grandfather had said – 'In the lap of the god?' He raised himself on his toes to look over the plump knees of the grotesque little idol. Yes, there it was – a leather bag, old and hardened, but still quite strong.

Dan, impatient with expectation, struggled to untie the stiff leather thong that secured it – a thong last tied by a highwayman long before Dan was born. At last it yielded and he tipped out a handful of gold coins – twenty or thirty gleaming sovereigns and pieces of jewellery with them – and the purse still held many times that number. Several hundred pounds must be contained in that little bag.

As Dan rode homeward through the growing dusk he thought with gratitude of his grandfather and his ill-fated boyhood friend. He remembered his words, 'If the money's still there it's yours to keep – may it bring you more happiness than it did young Tom Cranbrook.'

Happiness! Dan knew what that meant at this moment. Had his grandfather only known, he had given Dan that day the most wonderful black colt in the world, and had saved the whole family from anxiety for many a year to come.

Dan patted the glossy neck of Black Prince, as he stepped smoothly on into the darkness.

'No great gentleman's stables for you,' he smiled. 'You belong to me now.'

Bird of Battle

Lieutenant Jim Scott and the black eagle hawk joined the troop at the same time. It didn't take long for the men to make up their minds that their new commander and the sable bird were downright bad luck.

Then amid a welter of blood and violence and arrant mutiny Jim Scott proved that his men's fears were groundless.

From a sky the colour of dirty water, the cruel sun blazed down on a barren landscape – the Western Desert of 1942. The smooth sand-hills in the wadi were littered with the still smoking wreckage of war. The red hot shells of half a dozen German tanks were strewn over a half a mile, capsized and burning sullenly.

But to the British tank troop camped in the wadi, it was just another brief halt in the never-ending pursuit of Rommel's retreating Afrika Korps. In spite of their success during the last twenty-four hours it was a dark day for the weary figures sitting around their dusty tanks. A few hours before, Paddy Nelson, their beloved troop commander, had been killed by a stray bullet. Now a new troop commander was being sent from Tobruk and was due to arrive shortly.

It was 'Sunny' Dark, the Australian corporal, who summed up their feelings.

'Look at it this way,' he argued. 'Whoever we get is bound to be a drongo. Nobody had old Paddy's experience and know-how.'

'Shut up!' snapped Sergeant-Major Burton. 'Someone's got to take Nelson's place – and whoever he is, it's up to us to make him welcome.'

'Depends on what sort he is,' retorted Sunny. 'If he's one of them "death or glory" boys, he'll get the cold shoulder, if he's a good bloke . . . hello!' he broke off. 'Talk of the devil!'

Dragging a billowing cloud of dust behind it, a jeep had appeared over the level wastes and, a few minutes later, it reached the wadi.

The figure sitting beside the driver leapt out as it drew to a halt. He was a man of medium height, young, dark-haired and suntanned. He wore a rumpled Tank Corps uniform with an officer's cap.

The Sergeant-Major hurried forward and saluted.

'Glad to meet you, sir!' he said. 'I'm Sergeant-Major Burton. You'll be our new Troop Commander, Lieutenant Scott.'

'That's right, Sergeant,' Jim Scott replied. 'I've been with tanks since El Alamein, but I've never commanded a troop before, so I'll have to lean on you pretty heavily at first. Sorry to hear about Paddy Nelson. I believe he was one of the best.'

'He *was* one of the best, sir,' said Sunny Dark unsmilingly. 'We won't see his like again.'

Jim Scott caught the hostility behind the words, and tactfully he changed the subject.

'All tanks ready to move at dawn, Sergeant?'

'All present and correct, sir,' reported the Sergeant-Major. 'You'll be taking over Paddy . . . er . . . Lieutenant Nelson's tank.' He hesitated. 'That is, we can transfer you to something else if. . . .'

'I'll take over Paddy's tank,' Scott said easily. 'And how about some grub? I came straight from Tobruk and. . . .'

His words were cut short as a shadow floated over him. From the blank sky above, a silent form had drifted on silent wings to land on his shoulder. It was a small black eagle hawk, common enough in Libya.

'Hello, mate!' said Scott, grinning. He patted the bird's dusty plumage and it responded with a rusty croak. 'It looks tame enough,' he went on. 'Is this your troop mascot then?'

'Did you see that?' Sunny croaked in tones oddly like the bird's. 'It's taken to him!'

'Something peculiar about this,' Corporal Parker muttered. 'I've never known one of these hawks to settle on a man before.'

'It's quite simple, Corporal,' said Scott briskly. 'The Jerries were here for quite a time, you know. I expect they fed the bird scraps and tamed it so that it comes to anyone it sees.'

'Of course that must be it, sir,' agreed the Sergeant-Major loudly, and he turned to glare at the uneasy men. 'It's quite a reasonable theory.'

But if the explanation satisfied Sergeant Burton, it did little to soothe the qualms and fears of the men.

When Tanks Collide!

The next day dawned lowering and overcast. A brisk wind whipped up the sand into millions of microscopic grains which found their way into hair, mouths, mess tins and dixies.

Sunny Dark cursed savagely as a flurry of sand blew into his mug of tea for the tenth time.

'It's that flamin' bird,' he said bitterly. 'Nothing's gone right since it came. First old Paddy cops a bundle and now the weather changes. Look at it,' he added, squinting up to where the hawk was slowly circling the bivouac. 'It's deciding who it's going to pick on next.'

'It's picked the loot's tent,' one man said, as the bird dropped on top of the canvas. A harsh, unmusical shriek reached their ears.

The file-edged sound rasped on Sunny's already-raw nerves. He sprang to his feet, his red-rimmed eyes wild and staring.

'It's kept me awake all night,' he panted, snatching up his rifle. 'It's evil – that's what it is!'

With hands that trembled slightly, he sighted along his weapon. The rifle bucked and a badly-aimed bullet ripped through the top of the tent.

A moment later, Jim Scott erupted from the tent, a revolver in his hand, his eyes blazing. Behind him, came the Sergeant-Major.

'Who the blazes did that?' Scott cried.

'It . . . it's that darn hawk,' Sunny mumbled. 'It's gettin' on my nerves. I thought I'd have a crack at it and do it in for good!'

'Well, you can have a crack at Jerry instead!' said Scott grimly. 'A message from Base has just come through. Our troops in the Rififi Depression have been over-run by Jerry armour. Ten of their tanks punched a hole in our right flank and are heading this way. Let's go!'

In the bustle of departure, the incident of the bird was forgotten and soon the tanks were lurching up and down the sand dunes, Scott's vehicle in the lead, acting as point tank.

Jim Scott, standing in the turret, snapped down smoked goggles over his eyes and squinted ahead. It was not the weather conditions only that bothered him, but also the morale of his men.

'They've been out here too long,' he decided. 'They're all on edge and a trivial thing like that darned hawk worries them. What we need is a good smack at the Jerries and they'll have their tails in the air again!'

The Lieutenant called up Sergeant-Major Burton.

'Hello, Trumpet One Able. Looks like a sand-storm heading our way. Better form line abreast!'

Burton's solid, steady voice came back to him.

'Trumpet One Able! Jerries two o'clock to the right! Over!'

Hurriedly Scott shifted his field-glasses. Ahead of him through the wavering, shifting murk, he could see the dim shapes of crawling tanks.

'Jerries all right!' he confirmed. 'Okay, lads! Advance in line of battle and keep firing! Good luck! Out!'

Their engines roaring, the tanks leapt forward under full throttle. A spot of light blinked from the murk and Scott felt a ringing clang on the side of the tank. It reeled under the blast of the shell burst and Scott crouched down as shrapnel zigzagged a jagged path all round him.

He dropped inside the turret and spoke into his hand microphone.

'Tranverse right. Steady . . . on! Can you see it, gunner?'

'Got it, sir!'

'FIRE!'

The tank recoiled on its heavy springs as an armour-piercing shell hurtled from the gun barrel. Through his field-glasses, Scott saw a distant flash, then a slow, steady glow.

'A hit!' he yelled. 'A brew up!'

Then he was deafened by a tremendous concussion of noise as Burton, in the tank on his left, opened up. The German armour obviously not expecting to meet any resistance, scattered and disappeared.

Scott muttered impatiently as he scanned the battleground ahead. The tank they had knocked out glared red like a camp fire but now the sandstorm was coming down in a black cloud to destroy visibility. It was hard to decide whether the enemy had retreated or were going to continue the battle.

Then he heard a whistle overhead and an ear-shattering roar behind him. A voice yelled:

'We're brewed up, lads! Bale out!'

Scott made up his mind on the instant. To stay where they were would be suicide against the heavier German armament. Better to press ahead and hope to outflank the enemy.

'Trumpet One Able! Calling troop! Full throttle!'

The thirty tons of Scott's tank crested a sandhill and bore down the slope beyond. Scott was driving blind, looking for a break in the storm when suddenly something loomed up on his right.

'It can't be a Jerry!' he thought. 'We're still too far away!'

The other tank swerved towards them. Scott saw familiar markings and a white blur of face at the turret – Sergeant Burton!

'Left stick!' he shouted frantically.

The order came too late! With a grinding crunch, Scott's tank, travelling downhill, slewed into Burton's front track. For a moment, Scott looked straight into the Sergeant's shocked face, only feet away from his, then the other tank had tilted and crashed sideways.

The Tank-Men Mutiny

Scott flung down the microphone and leaped from the turret. As he fought his way through the screaming, sand-laden wind, he saw that Burton's crew had managed to free themselves from the overturned tank. But the Sergeant-Major, his face chalk-white, lay sprawled on his back, one arm dangling.

Together, they supported Burton back to Scott's tank and lowered the faintly moaning man inside. Five minutes later, the co-driver popped his head out to announce:

'He's got a broken arm and cracked ribs, sir. We've given him a pain-killing injection!'

Scott nodded dumbly and with the other members of Burton's crew he crouched down beside the tank to await the end of the storm. It took half an hour – an eternity of shrieking winds and knife-edged sand before the gale finally blew itself out.

As the light brightened, Scott stretched his cramped limbs and staggered to his feet, looking for his lost tanks.

He found them close behind him, spread out in irregular formation across the desert. At first, they resembled new dunes sprung up during the storm. Then as their engines started, the clinging weight of sand fell away and slowly the monsters lumbered towards him.

As the men dismounted from their tanks, Scott saw the same numb expression on their faces. One thought was all in their minds – the bad luck that dogged them had struck again!

Two men made a quick inspection of the tanks and reported back to Scott.

'They've thrown their tracks and can't be moved. We'll have to radio base and get the REME up here for a repair job.'

'All right, men,' Scott said briskly. 'Back to your own tanks. Jerry has cleared off so we'll head for our positions and find out what the situation is. Sharp now!'

An hour later, they reached the British positions.

A battle-stained infantry Lieutenant scrambled out of one of the slit trenches and ran to Scott.

'Am I glad to see you lot!' he cried. 'We had a heck of a sandstorm a little while back and in the middle of it, the Jerry tanks came charging back and overran us. They headed off to their own lines, but they'll be back!'

'We've already met 'em,' said Scott and quickly he explained the situation.

'Tough luck!' sympathised the Lieutenant. 'But you've still got seven tanks left. What's the drill? Do you want to dig in hull down to support us or make an all-out attack in front?'

Scott licked his cracked, sand-dried lips.

'Leave it to me,' he said, picking his words carefully. 'I'll have a word with my blokes and let you know the form.'

'Suits me,' said the Lieutenant turning away. 'But I wouldn't waste much time – Jerry won't! See you later!'

Slowly, Scott crunched across the sand towards his tanks. He gave a mirthless chuckle as he saw them. The tanks were all right, he told himself, but it was the crews. . . . He stopped, gaping.

Behind his own vehicle, stood Corporal Parker. He had his revolver out, the hammer cocked. He was bending down, the mouth of his pistol pressed against one foot.

'Parker!' shouted Scott.

With a guilty start, the man straightened and whipped his revolver out of sight behind his back.

'I'm putting you on a charge, Corporal,' gritted Scott. 'Cowardice in the face of the enemy. Caught in the act of inflicting a wound on yourself so you'll dodge a bit of fighting!'

'Go ahead!' said Parker sullenly. 'Put me on a charge and see what good it does you. You'll find the rest of our blokes think the same!'

Red rage filled Scott's mind and he took an impulsive pace forward.

Instantly, Parker brought his hand out with the pistol levelled.

'Keep back!' he yelled hysterically. 'I'm not going to be killed for you or anyone. . . .'

At that moment, Sunny Dark stepped into view between two tanks, the other crews behind him.

'Parker's right, sir,' he said quietly. 'And we're with him. We're not going on any suicide mission with that bird hanging around!'

Following the direction of his pointing finger, Scott saw the black eagle hawk sitting on the muzzle of a tank gun, preening its feathers.

'You're mad, all of you!' he gasped. 'Afraid of going into battle because of a stupid bird. . . .' Sheer anger made him fall silent.

'It's easy enough to talk,' said Sunny evenly. 'But ever since you and that bird joined us, we've run into strife.' He pointed at an ambulance which was speeding back from the forward positions. 'There goes the old sarge – one of the best blokes in the world – and the only one who could have got us out of this mess. Look what happened to him! Sorry sir, but we're refusing to obey any further orders!'

There was a murmur of agreement from the other men and Scott wiped his brow, his thoughts rioting. What he and every officer had always dreaded had come to pass. Mutiny!

It was then that the infantry officer ran on the scene. Cheerfully, he pushed his way through the knot of sullen men and burst into speech.

'Jerry's getting ready for a big push,' he said breathlessly. 'I reckon you tankies will need all the luck you can get. What's the idea of the bird, by the way? Sort of a good luck mascot, eh?'

'Good luck . . .' began Scott bitterly and then he stopped as suddenly he saw his way clear. 'That's it, Lieutenant,' he continued calmly. 'You're quite right. The bird is our good luck sign.' He took a deep breath and raised his voice. 'All right men, you've got your orders. I'll lead the way and the rest of you will follow!'

He snatched up the flag of the Tank Corps from one of the tanks and turned to the officer.

'My tank's been knocked out,' he said. 'Have you got any wheeled transport with you?'

'Well, there's my old staff car,' the Lieutenant said hesitatingly. 'When I say "wheeled," it's got four wheels and they go round, but that's about all!'

He gestured to a small, dilapidated saloon car nearby with a cracked and hanging hood.

'Just the job!' said Scott. 'I'd like to borrow it and a driver as well!'

'It's yours!' the Lieutenant said, waving to one of his men to join them.

'But I don't quite see the idea.'

'Shock tactics!' said Scott tersely.

He did not explain that his tactics were designed to shock his own men and not the enemy! He slid into the front seat beside the driver, a chunky fair-haired private. He held the flag of the Tank Corps proudly on high and yelled:

'All right, James! Step on it!'

The driver gave one puzzled glance at his officer, shrugged and then stepped on it! The car bounded towards the enemy lines, leaving the tank crews staring in baffled astonishment.

'The loot's gone troppo!' said Sunny uneasily, his eyes fixed on the bounding car. 'He must have a touch of the sun!'

'Hey, look!' shouted Parker. 'The bird's following him!'

All eyes turned on the hawk which rose from the gun barrel and winged its way behind the staff car. The troops, under the Lieutenant's orders, were scrambling out of their trenches to form up on a start line at one side.

'If those boys go in ahead of us,' Parker cried, 'they'll get clobbered for sure!'

For the first time that day, the tank crews met one another's eyes and read the same message there – shame and guilt!

'We can't have that!' Sunny Dark shouted. 'Come on, what are we standing here for? Let's get weaving!'

Machine Gun Menace

One by one, the tanks ground into gear and lurched forward, slowly at first and then more quickly as the engines rose to a crescendo of power. Behind them, swarmed the British infantry.

Ahead of them in the bouncing staff car, Scott shouted in his driver's ear:

'We'll leave the others behind! Slow down!'

'Suits me, mate!' grunted the soldier. 'I'm no bloomin' hero!'

'We've caught 'em off balance!' he shouted. 'Looks like they were massing their infantry and armour for an attack!'

But Lieutenant Scott was not listening. He had heard the noise he was waiting for – the growling roar of tank engines! A proud grin split his face as he looked behind and saw his tank troop following him into battle.

By now, the 75mm. shells from the British guns were hurtling over his head with the sound of express trains. Scott saw one German tank explode as a shell landed clean under its tracks. Another German tank was hit by an armour-piercing shell and the infantry clinging to the back, scurried like ants from the blazing wreck.

Then a grenade landed close by the car's wheels. The vehicle rose in the air as if a giant's hand had lifted it like a toy. Scott was slung sideways and landed on soft sand.

As he picked himself up, half-dazed, he saw the driver scrambling to his feet.

'Holy smoke!' he cried. 'That was close. . . .'

Then he spun round and fell as a burst of machine gun fire took him in the shoulder. Scott saw the pock marks of another burst racing towards him and felt a hard blow on his side. He dropped on his face beside the overturned car. Hastily, he felt his side and found that a ricochet had only bruised his ribs.

At one side, he saw three Germans manning a machine gun from the shelter of a burnt-out truck. Thinking they had disposed of him, the machine gun had swung its arc and was now spraying the advancing British troops.

Scott took a deep breath and, crouching low, he raced from the car towards the machine gun nest. Two bullets from his revolver ripped into the shelter and one of the Germans turned his head to see Scott only yards away.

He gave a yell of fear and flung up his hands. His companion did the same, but the machine gunner was made of sterner stuff.

He swung the muzzle until it loomed at Scott like the mouth of a tunnel. Then a diving form swooped from the sky. It shot past the Lieutenant's face and instinctively, he flinched. That action saved his life as, a split second later, a deadly burst of lead ripped over his shoulder.

Scott saw the hawk dive on past him, its raking claws slashing at the German's face. The German flung up one hand to fend off the razor-sharp claws and beating wings. In that instant, Scott found his wits and levelled his revolver. He fired and the German slid over his gun, a bullet in his head.

Ten minutes later, Scott was standing guard over his prisoners with the aid of the wounded driver. Then the infantry officer came running to join him.

'Great show, Scott!' he shouted. 'We've beaten 'em hands down and they're pulling out!' He gazed in astonishment at the black bird perched on Scott's shoulder. 'Good grief!' he gasped. 'Are you training birds to fight the Jerries now?'

'That's right!' agreed Scott. 'Now if you'll look after these two beauties, I'll get back to my tanks.'

'No need for that!' cried the Lieutenant as Sunny Dark's tank came loom-

Scott saw the hawk drive on past him, its raking claws slashing at the German's face.

ing through the smoke.

'Hi ya, skipper!' waved Sunny from the turret. 'How about a lift?'

'Does that include my friend as well?' Scott grinned.

'Too right!' Sunny yelled cheerfully.

Tired as he was, Scott's heart was light as he climbed on to the back of the tank. He snatched up Sunny's hand microphone and broadcast to his troop.

'Hello, Trumpet One Able. Your Troop Commander speaking! Thanks a lot, lads! I was afraid when I first took over, you lot were going to give me the bird!'

Scott grinned as he heard the shout of laughter coming back from his men. For they were now once more, his men and his friends – thanks to the bird of battle!

The Spanish Doubloon

Captain Thomas Mountjoy stared down at the half-drowned man sprawled on the deck of the English frigate. That the senseless man was an enemy Spaniard was plain to see, one of those who had sailed with the doomed Great Armada.

Then Thomas saw the medallion that dangled from the Spaniard's neck. It was a semi-circle of gold, half a Spanish doubloon and for the English sea-captain it had a special significance.

'Pedro, where are you?' shouted Thomas, as he ran along the echoing cloisters of Hampton Court. A group of richly dressed courtiers turned to protest at the unseemly noise.

'Drake is landed at Plymouth!' the boy called to them as he passed. 'Drake is home!'

'How comes this news?' said one of the courtiers, a tall dark man in the black doublet and cloak of the Spanish court.

'From Lord Mountjoy, my father, sir. He had it from his own messenger this morning,' answered the boy.

As the babble of conversation broke out Thomas escaped and ran on and out into the great Yew Walk, still calling 'Pedro!'

There was a snapping of twigs and a tearing sound as another boy, taller than Thomas and eleven years to his ten, scrambled out from one of the yew trees, shaking its venerable branches as he swung to the ground. The younger boy giggled as he thought of the contrast between the dusty dishevelled figure before him in its sagging hose and torn breeches, and the stiff formally

As Thomas sank, he felt his hair grasped and saw Pedro's face close to his own.

dressed young man who followed His Excellency the Spanish Ambassador into the Queen's presence each morning.

'Drake's ship has her hold full of treasure,' he said proudly. 'Gold taken from you Spaniards, too, and the sailors have many strange tales to tell.'

'I, too, have heard this news,' said Pedro. 'Our Ambassador has good spies everywhere. On Sunday, when the ships were sighted off Plymouth, the townspeople were at church, but before the priest finished his sermon, he spoke to an empty church for they had all gone to see Drake.'

A look of sadness came over Pedro's thin brown face as he added: 'But, you know, amigo, we are now enemies. His Excellency will return home to Cadiz and I with him.'

'Then I shall have to hide you somewhere in the Palace,' said Thomas.

Later that day, Thomas stood before his father, Lord Mountjoy. 'My son,' said the Earl wearily, 'Pedro is a Spaniard and as such, though not yet an enemy, can scarcely be called a friend. It is, therefore, my wish that your meetings with Pedro de Salvador should cease altogether. The Spaniards will not stay in England now that Drake has humiliated them and will sail within the week, Pedro with them.' The Earl sighed as he saw the sullen expression on the boy's face. ' 'Tis hard, I know, but you will shortly be a man and must learn to endure.'

The next two days went drearily for the boy. He avoided his tutor and classes, staying all day by the river to watch the ceremonial barges. These came and went constantly between the City of London and Hampton Court, carrying high ranking visitors to see the Queen, or not to see her, according to her mood. Once he found himself near to Pedro on the jetty and tried to attract his attention but the Spanish boy was pulled sharply away by one of his own countrymen and Thomas realised that Pedro, too, had been warned of the dangers of having friends among the enemy.

There was a fair crowd on the banks and their attention was caught at that moment by the commotion on a barge in the middle of the river. It was clear that the craft was leaking badly as the oarsmen were baling water with their hats, for want of any other baling equipment, and a portly alderman in the stern was threatening to overturn the boat as well as he danced about shouting for help. Thomas turned to get a better view and caught his foot suddenly in an iron mooring-ring. In a flash he had toppled over the side of the jetty and plunged into the river. Like most well-born children of his time, Thomas could not swim a stroke and he thrashed wildly about with his arms, the water choking his cries. His waterlogged clothes dragged him under, but as he sank, he felt his hair grasped and saw Pedro's face close to his own.

'Help! Help!' yelled Pedro, and soon many hands were pulling them out on to the jetty. Both boys grinned at each other as they lay gasping for breath. Spanish and English onlookers bowed formally to each other, thanks were exchanged and each boy was led away in a different direction.

At the end of the week his father sent for Thomas. 'I have business in Tilbury and I wish you to accompany me.'

'As you wish, sir,' said Thomas doubtfully. He did not dare to tell his father that he wanted to stay at the Palace to see his friend leave.

'Besides,' the Earl continued, 'I have heard that the Spanish ships will be sailing from there on the afternoon tide.'

Thomas, overjoyed, realised that his father was giving him the opportunity of seeing Pedro set sail on the Ambassador's galleon, and a look of understanding passed between father and son.

The docks were aswarm with shipping and the sky over the river was latticed with the rigging of tall masts. The quayside was thronged with sailors and stevedores bustling about their business. Out in the river great first raters swung to their anchor chains, while armed merchant vessels passed up and down. Here and there a few lean privateers could be seen loading powder and shot. The boy stared at these ships, for they were all so different from the broad galleons with their high ornate castles at either end, which he had often seen before. The Earl, too, was staring at them.

'Aye, Thomas, they are new and strange indeed. Look at the number of guns they carry!'

'There they lie!' Thomas pointed to the high gilded sterns of the Spanish ships, and would have run towards them if his father had not laid a restraining hand on his shoulder.

'What crowded decks! Do they need so many hands for sailing?' asked Thomas.

'No,' replied his father, 'the Spanish ships carry a number of soldiers as well as sailors so that when they grapple an enemy they can quickly despatch him.'

By the shouts and bustle on board it was obvious that the two galleons were sailing shortly. Suddenly Thomas spotted a familiar figure waving frantically from the forecastle high above. 'Thomas!' he called excitedly, 'I am so glad that you have come.' Before Thomas could reply, the Spanish boy ducked down from the rail and reappeared a moment later waving something at his friend. 'Catch!' he cried. 'I have the other half!' A small leather pouch fell at Thomas's feet. He opened it and pulled out a semi-circle of gold.

'Why, 'tis half a doubloon,' he explained 'and with letters on it.' The boy and his father peered closely and made out the letters THOM engraved over the design on one face and RO on the other side. The Earl smiled.

'Pedro has put your name and his own on this coin, as an emblem of your friendship.'

The Spanish ship was already gliding from the quayside, as Thomas waved goodbye and shouted that he would look after the keepsake for ever.

As they made their way back to where the groom was holding their horses Lord Mountjoy said quietly: 'For your next birthday, my son, I will mount your doubloon on a gold chain.'

The Armada

In the years that followed the gold chain and half-doubloon accompanied Thomas Mountjoy on many exciting adventures. Together they sailed round the world with Francis Drake, and Thomas earned a share of the great treasure in gold and silver bars which the *Golden Hind* brought back to Plymouth. He gained yet more prize money on voyages to the West Indies.

In the spring of the year 1588 he arrived back in England, a comparatively wealthy man. For a long time now there had been rumours of a second Armada being prepared to sail against England. In May the King of Spain confirmed the rumours by issuing a full description of his 'most happy Armada' and its invincible strength. At the news, beacons were built across the whole breadth of England and vessels, many of them privately commissioned by noblemen out of their own pockets, were fitted out hastily with men and ammunition.

Thomas, by this time an experienced naval officer, was eager to defend his country from the new danger. Using his prize money he commissioned a small but fast frigate, the *Advantage*. News came that the Spanish fleet had sailed on the first of June but had then been turned back by storms. Thomas carried on with his preparations and in a few weeks was able to put to sea. Following the example set by Drake, he embarked on a training cruise and sailed slowly down the Channel.

On the night of the nineteenth of July, Thomas was woken by the officer of the watch.

'The beacons are lit, sir, all along the coast!'

Thomas ordered full sail for Plymouth, where he expected to find the English fleet. On the way he put in at Newhaven. Sloops had been in that day with information on the position of the two fleets and the progress of the battle. The *Advantage* was loaded to capacity with fresh supplies of shot and powder for the English and Thomas brought his ship out of harbour to join the battle.

'Sails ho!' cried the lookout. Thomas sprang up the rigging and saw hundreds of sails studding the horizon. As the wind dropped he brought his frigate up to join the rear of the English flotilla. All night long small boats laden with supplies plied to and fro between the *Advantage* and the English ships.

As day broke Thomas took his own vessel into battle, and heard the sound of Spanish shot whistling through his rigging. In the confusion and eddying acrid smoke came news that a Spanish galleon was taken. The spasmodic fighting died away as night fell, and the Armada made for the shelter of Calais, with the little English ships in silent pursuit. Off Calais the Spaniards anchored in close formation, while the English still harried them from behind.

About midnight Thomas heard the muffled creak of oars and a voice from the darkness hailed: 'Ship ahoy!'

'Frigate *Advantage,*' replied the officer of the watch. A boat drew into the faint light cast by the ship's lantern.

'Load all guns and run them out ready for firing,' came the order and the boat slid away back into the darkness. Thomas gave the necessary orders and then went below to snatch an hour's sleep.

Before dawn the mate woke him.

'Fireships, sir, sailing into the enemy fleet!' In an instant Thomas caught up his spy-glass and ran on deck. The sea was lit by eight blazing barques, now almost among the Spanish fleet. He could see the alarm and confusion spreading among the enemy vessels as sails were quickly run up. Here and there a panic-stricken ship's crew cut its anchor cable before hoisting sail and drifted helplessly through the Armada. The other ships tacked from the shore in every possible direction, breaking up the tight-knit formation. To add to the confusion, the English opened fire as soon as their targets were within range.

When dawn broke, the mighty Spanish fleet was divided into two bodies, vainly trying to regroup.

'Look, Captain,' called the mate, 'there is a galliasse aground on the sands. Shall we join them there and get some plunder?'

'Nay,' cried Thomas. 'Bring her round. We fight before plundering.' Helped by the wind and tide they rapidly moved into the thick of the fray.

The stern of a great Spanish galleon loomed suddenly above them, out of the smoke.

'Bear her in close,' roared Thomas, and a full broadside blasted the side of the Spaniard as it slid by. Smoke billowed, hiding the fall of their shot, but they could hear the crashing of timbers and screaming as their salvo took effect. The Don's guns thundered a volley in return. Thomas, through the smoke, saw a tangle of falling rigging but the frigate still rode well and the enemy slipped away astern and was lost in the smoke.

As the afternoon wore on the wind freshened, blowing away the cloud of gunsmoke and revealing a scene of destruction. For the tenth time the *Advantage* attacked an enemy ship. Amidst the carnage on their decks the Spaniards were valiantly preparing to attempt to board the frigate.

'Take her aback,' thundered Thomas, and the ship shuddered to a stop broadside on to the enemy.

'Will they never learn?' he thought, as grappling irons snaked across from the enemy ship and fell short into the water. His own broadside drowned the rest of these thoughts.

'All hands down from the rigging,' he gave the order, and in a lower voice to the mate: 'At this short range the Don can only hit above our decks.'

By now the gun crews of the *Advantage* were returning two broadsides for every one fired by the enemy.

'They must strike their flag soon,' the mate muttered.

'Surrender!' Thomas called across to the other side. The only reply was a musket ball that took away his hat.

Descending to the gun deck, he now gave an order to the gun master. 'Round shot only and double-shot the guns, Master Smith. We shall send them to the bottom.'

The weary gunners and powder-monkeys raised a hoarse cheer at these words. Thomas continued down the decks to see the wounded. When he returned to the quarter-deck the mate greeted him with 'They will not last long now, sir.' Thomas saw the Spanish ship wallowing in the choppy seas.

'The devils are firing yet!' cried the mate, and even as the galleon rolled over in her last agonies, a solitary gun boomed its defiance at the English.

Then the great ship slowly slid under. The sea was littered with dead bodies, broken spars and a few survivors struggling for their lives. The weary powder-blackened crew of the *Advantage* raised a ragged cheer and then set about raising jury rigging to repair the heavy damage wrought aloft by the sunken Spaniard's guns.

A struggling knot of sailors caught Thomas's attention. With drawn sword he strode over to investigate. As he neared the group he saw the dripping body of a Spaniard being hauled on to the deck by two sailors, while the third, a huge bearded man, stood with upraised knife about to strike.

'Hold!' yelled Thomas. 'What have you there?'

' 'Tis but a Spaniard, Captain,' growled the bearded man reluctantly lowering the knife.

'I'll have no cold-blooded murder aboard my ship,' commanded Thomas. 'Every man, be he Don or English has fought bravely this day.' The look of disappointment on the sailor's face prompted him to add: 'Why save him; only to kill?' Two of the sailors looked sheepish, but the third blurted out: 'Sir, we saw gold on him as he drifted past.'

'Ho, a little private plundering! Let us see this gold.' Thomas turned the unconscious Spaniard over with this foot. He was a handsome man of Thomas's own age with a heavy black moustache and beard. The Spaniard stirred a little as Thomas lifted a heavy gold chain from around his neck and held it up to the waning light. With a shock of recognition he saw the matching half to his own doubloon. With a startled oath he turned to the three sailors and in a voice filled with emotion said: 'This Spaniard once saved my life. Take him below and give him every attention.'

The rescued man lay in the captain's cot looking exhausted but defiant, when Thomas entered the cabin. Without a word he laid the Spanish gold chain on the blanket, and then still without a word smilingly laid his own chain beside it. For a moment the man stared uncomprehendingly at the two halves of the doubloon, then he smiled weakly.

'Thomas, is it truly you?'

'Aye, Pedro, my old friend, 'tis truly me.'

Later, when Pedro was more recovered the two friends talked.

The remains of the Armada, after one final vain attempt to attack, had turned and the battered ships now fled before a full gale to try to make their escape around Scotland. The howling of the wind in the rigging and the crack of the ship nearly drowned the voice of the two friends as they told each other their adventures. When Thomas heard of Pedro's wife and child in Spain he came to a decision.

'I cannot surrender you as a prisoner-of-war,' he said. 'I am forced to seek shelter off the coast of France from the gale. When it dies down 'twill be an easy matter to land you on that coast.'

In the early light a small boat left the side of the *Advantage*. The same three sailors who had tried to kill Pedro now rowed the pair to the French shore.

After many farewells, Thomas thrust a purse of gold on his friend and

Pedro jumped ashore, calling over his shoulder: 'Goodbye, amigo. With the help you have given me I shall soon be in Spain again.'

'Wait, Pedro, wait! You never surrendered and yet you have no sword. Wear mine with honour in memory of a noble battle.' Thomas unbuckled his own sword and threw it on to the shingle. As the boat slipped quietly out to sea Thomas heard Pedro's voice calling out above the sound of the waves: 'I hope in a happier time our gold doubloon will be reunited again.'